Snow Summer

Snow Summer
Kit Peel

Groundwood Books
House of Anansi Press
Toronto Berkeley

Published in Canada and the USA in 2016 by Groundwood Books

Groundwood Books / House of Anansi Press
groundwoodbooks.com

With the participation of the Government of Canada | Canadä
Avec la participation du gouvernement du Canada

Library and Archives Canada Cataloguing in Publication
Peel, Kit, author
Snow summer / Kit Peel.
Issued also in electronic formats.
ISBN 978-1-55498-357-5 (bound).—ISBN 978-1-55498-359-9
(html).—ISBN 978-1-55498-358-2 (mobi)
I. Title.
PZ7.1.P44Sn 2016   j823'.92   C2015-908448-2
C2015-908449-0

Jacket illustration © Tim Zeltner, i2iart.com
Design by Michael Solomon

Groundwood Books is committed to protecting our natural environment. As part of our efforts, the interior of this book is printed on paper that contains 100% post-consumer recycled fibers, is acid-free and is processed chlorine-free.

Printed and bound in Canada

MIX
Paper from
responsible sources
FSC
www.fsc.org   FSC® C016245

For Megan, Awen and Paloma

Ah! as the heart grows older
It will come to such sights colder

"Spring and Fall"
Gerard Manley Hopkins

1

"You coming?" Kate asked her sister.

She was holding open a gate by the side of the road. Although it was nearly the end of the summer holidays, snow gleamed on the top bar of the gate, in the branches of a tree over Kate's head and all across the meadow behind and the dale beyond, all the way up to the hilltops where it gave way to a bright blue sky.

Lisa, Kate's older sister, hung back on the pavement. Wyn was already in the meadow, tying on her snowshoes. She tightened the last strap and glanced up, meeting Lisa's glare.

"I'll see you two at home," said Lisa.

"Suit yourself," said Wyn. With a quick movement she tugged the gate out of Kate's grip, slamming it shut.

Lisa headed off briskly, catching up with a group of friends whose faces were muffled in scarves and woolly hats. Their breaths left puffs of white in the cold air.

"Well, that was friendly," said Kate, rolling her eyes at Wyn.

"She wasn't coming, was she?"

"People skills, Wyn. We've spoken about this. If you're nice to someone, they might be nice back."

"She was in a mood."

"You're going to tell me you don't know why?"

"Like I care?"

"You're going to tell me that you didn't notice that a certain boy, who Lisa has been into for ages, spent quite a long time hanging around you in the pool just now?"

"It was only John," said Wyn. "And I'm not encouraging him or anything."

"No?"

"No."

"But you were talking to him."

"So I can't talk to John now?"

"Since when do you ever talk to anyone at school?"

"I talk to you."

"What am I going to do with you?" said Kate.

"You don't have to do anything."

Together they set off into the freezing white field, their snowshoes leaving lattice prints behind them. Drifts had formed in the middle of the field, coming up almost to Wyn's waist. Kate plowed through them, panting with the effort. When an icy wind blew off the moors and down into the dale, Kate complained and rubbed her arms. Wyn quickly rubbed her arms, too, and pretended her teeth were chattering.

A little way ahead, clustered along the bank of the river Nidd, was a mass of branches and brambles, rigid with ice and snow. Kate stopped, squinting at a movement in the thicket.

"I think I just saw a swallow," she said, now hurrying forward as fast as the deep snow would let her. "I'm sure it was. If they're back, it means we're going to have summer! Finally!"

But even as Kate was floundering excitedly forward, Wyn's eyes pierced the thicket and saw the bird that was hopping about within it. She was wondering whether to tell the other girl the truth, when the bird broke cover, heading updale along the river, where it joined with two other similar birds. Kate ground to a halt, staring sadly after them.

"Just blackbirds," she said, before brightening with a new hope. "Come on, there's still the river to check."

Wyn followed her to a gap in the thicket beyond which there was an iron bridge. They scrambled up the riverbank, their snowshoes awkward on the slope. Halfway across the bridge, they stopped and examined the river Nidd, searching in vain for any trickle of life. It was solid ice all the way down to the mud bed. The little family of fish that Wyn and Kate stared at every day were just where they'd left them, frozen in their never-ending conversation.

"I'm still convinced that when the Nidd melts, the deep-freeze family will all come back to life and start swimming away," said Kate. "Do you think the Nidd will melt this year?"

Wyn knew how much Kate, with her water-blue eyes, loved to swim in the river. Last summer, in the brief weeks of color and warmth, Kate had insisted on picnicking by the Nidd nearly every day.

"Who knows," Wyn murmured.

The two girls walked on in silence until the white roofs of the village of Pateley Bridge came into sight and they were stepping onto a salted road. Wyn and Kate stopped to take off their snowshoes, then crunched up the back high street, past the Dales rescue office, with its heavily equipped orange Land Rovers parked outside, and on uphill past St. Cuthbert's church, its freshly painted red door a rare flash of color in the monochrome surroundings.

After the church, on the outskirts of the village, they turned onto the steep lane that led to Highdale House, Kate's family home. For the past three years, it had also been Wyn's home.

The long, low shape of the house came into view above the high walls of the lane. Snow washed over the roof. Icicles hung from the drainpipes, sparkling in the sun. A thick trail of wood smoke rose from the chimney. In the woods to the left of the farm, a fight had broken out among the resident jackdaws. Wyn watched more of the birds swoop down from the moors, chattering noisily as they touched down on frosty branches.

As they went higher up the lane, more of Nidderdale came into view. Except for the gray of houses, tree trunks and the old stone walls, everything lay white and muffled with cold. It was the same story in the next dale, the one beyond that and on and on, across continents and oceans.

For as long as Wyn and Kate had been alive, the world's weather had been changing. Every year, all across the world, snow had started falling earlier and earlier, and had lasted longer and longer. Now, deep into summer, it still showed no sign of melting. This year weather forecasters were predicting that the icy weather wouldn't break at all; it would be a summer of snow. And nobody understood why.

2

❖❖❖❖

Kate's mother, Joan Hebden, was standing at the front
door with her back to them, her hair as long and almost
as blonde as her daughters'. She was holding a paintbrush,
which she'd just dipped in emerald-colored paint.

"She's, like, turning into some crazy painting lady. Every
church door in the dale and now our house," whispered
Kate, before calling out to her mother, "Hey, Ma, the
school's looking like it needs a repaint, too."

Joan put the brush in a pot of turpentine and with her
foot scraped the green-flecked snow from the door. She
frowned when she saw them.

"Lisa's not with you?" she said.

"She took the long way home," said Kate. She headed
inside, kicking off her boots.

Joan followed her. Wyn hung up her coat, took off her
boots and tidied Kate's, then stepped into the sitting room.
A wood-burning stove, packed with logs, burned fiercely

in the hearth. She had intended to cross the room and join the others in the kitchen, but instead, quite against her will, she found herself rooted to the spot in front of the stove's glass door. In the last few months, the stove had begun to cast a strange power over her, by turns unsettling and exciting her. And today the pull of the dancing flames was even stronger than before. She felt them reaching out to her, all burning fingers and wild whispers, wanting her to open the door that held them captive. With the greatest of efforts, Wyn stepped away from the flames, but as she did, the logs in the stove shifted and fell against the stove door, pushing it open. A burning log tumbled from the stove and across the room towards her. It settled on the rug, just by her foot. Flames washed over the rug's tassels, setting them alight.

Grabbing a pair of tongs from the hearth, Wyn reached out to the log, intending to throw it back into the stove. Instead, she found herself unable to move, transfixed by the flames that rose up towards her. Their voices were clearer now and more insistent. She tried to close the tongs around the log, but couldn't. When she tried to call for help, her breath stuck in her throat. She could only stand there, feeling the heat of the fire grow around her.

Lisa burst in from the porch. Snatching up the tongs, she tossed the log back into the stove and stamped out the flames from the rug.

"What the hell were you doing?" Lisa demanded.

Joan and Kate rushed through from the kitchen. Seeing the scorched rug, Joan went to fetch a bowl of water. She returned and set about the rug.

"What happened?" said Joan.

"She was just watching a log burning the rug and doing nothing about it," said Lisa.

"I wasn't," retorted Wyn.

"Don't give me that. I know what I saw."

"Well, everything is fine now," said Joan. "We'll cut off the tassels and no one will be the wiser."

"Why do you always defend her?" said Lisa. She stormed into the porch, pulling on boots and heading outside. Joan asked where she was going.

"A long way from here," said Lisa, slamming the front door. Joan went after her.

Kate went into the kitchen, returning with a pair of scissors that she used to snip the burned tassels. Wyn retreated from the fire and paced on the far side of the room.

"There. Nobody would ever know." Kate stood up and admired her handiwork.

"It's not my fault the door wasn't shut properly," said Wyn.

"Nobody is saying it is."

"She's just having her revenge because she didn't want to walk back with us."

"I don't think she is."

"Why are you taking her side?"

"I'm not, I'm ..." Kate stepped forward and wrapped her arms around Wyn, who tried to push her friend away. Kate would not let go, though, until Wyn had stopped shaking.

For the past three years, Kate had been Wyn's calm waters. On the first night Wyn had been brought to Highdale, near-hysterical at what had happened to her first foster mother, Kate had come into Wyn's new bedroom, refusing to leave no matter how much Wyn raged at her. Kate had stayed the night with her, sitting on the floor until, at dawn, Wyn had finally fallen asleep. That had been the pattern of Wyn's first weeks at Highdale, until cracks of light had begun to seep into Wyn's defenses of anger and silence. Kate and Wyn began walking to school together; Wyn saying little, just listening to Kate's animated chatter. Until then, Wyn had refused to make a single friend at school.

Now, despite her best efforts, she had let herself grow close to this popular, outspoken girl. Whenever the nightmares woke Wyn, Kate would come to her, and Wyn had stopped pushing her away.

The Reverend Robin Hebden came home as evening was reddening the sky and wood smoke and mist hung across the dale. He stamped his feet for longer than necessary in the porch, sighing and muttering until Kate couldn't stand it any longer and demanded that her father tell her what was wrong.

"David Ramsgill's got the go-ahead from the council," said Robin. "He's going to quarry Skrikes Wood."

Over dinner, Robin told them how he'd heard the news that afternoon and had gone to see John's father, David Ramsgill, who owned the big quarry on the other side of the dale. Robin had begged him to leave Skrikes Wood alone.

"And he wouldn't listen to you?" said Joan.

"He says the wood is sitting on a rich vein of limestone, which the council is desperate for. I tried my best to make him see sense. Then John burst in on us, taking my side against his father. Not something that David Ramsgill appreciated. I do hope John's not in too much trouble on my account."

"Good for John," said Kate, flashing a look at Wyn.

"But Skrikes Wood has been a nature reserve forever. Surely it's protected," said Joan.

"Was protected," said Robin.

"I don't understand what everyone is getting so worked up about. The wood's dead, so what does it matter if it's dug up?" asked Lisa.

"Skrikes Wood is not dead," said Robin.

"Then it's on its last legs, like everything else in the dale. I don't know why we're still here. We could be in London, or some other city. Somewhere there's some life, some place we don't have to go round painting doors bright colors to cheer us all up. We don't have to be stuck here, in the back of beyond, living in black and white."

Suddenly Robin slammed his hand on the table. The plates and cutlery jumped. Joan had to grab her glass before it tipped over.

For a moment everyone sat in stunned silence. Even Robin seemed taken aback by what he'd just done.

"I'm sorry, there was no call for that," he said.

"When does the digging start?" asked Joan.

"In a few days, I think."

"How deep will they go?"

"Deep enough."

"Have you told…?"

"Not yet," said Robin, giving Joan a warning look.

Heavy snow was falling past the windowpanes when the Hebden family and Wyn moved to the sitting room to watch the evening news.

To save oil, the central heating was off now and wouldn't come on until the morning. The sitting room, with its wood-burning stove, was now the only really warm room in the house. Robin, Joan and Lisa sat lined up in a row on the sofa close to the hearth, Lisa tapping on her cell phone. Wyn was curled up in an armchair at the back of the room, as far away as possible from the fire. Kate sat on a cushion on the floor, between Wyn and her family.

When the news came on, the family watched in frowning silence. Yet another war was breaking out, this time in east Africa. It was the same story all over again; crops failing in the cold and water reserves frozen. People were on the move, but there was nowhere to move to. The second story was from Russia, where the army had set up checkpoints stopping people from pouring from the harsh countryside into a big city. A third story came on about bears and wolves coming over the frozen seas into Scotland. Wyn watched the man on the TV pausing by a fir tree and pointing out the scratch marks on the trunk.

The news ended with reports that vast snowstorms were developing at both the North and the South Poles. Satellite images appeared on the screen, showing how quickly the storms were spreading. One weather forecaster speculated that these storms might spread worldwide, and somehow Wyn knew that the forecaster was right. These giant snowstorms were growing in power second by second. And the thought of them covering the world made Wyn angry. She ground her fingers into the chair as anger washed over her; anger at the storm, anger that nobody was doing anything to stop it. Her head throbbed and a voice whispered something to her, over and over. She couldn't make out what the voice was saying, only that it wanted something from her.

Suddenly Kate's face appeared in front of her, asking something.

"What?" cried Wyn.

The word had come out so loudly that Robin, Joan and Lisa all turned around.

Lisa was about to say something when the TV made a popping noise. At the same time, the house lights went off.

With the efficiency acquired from living through so many blackouts, everyone set to work. Candles were lit. Glass lanterns were placed over bright flames. Carrying a lantern, Wyn went into the kitchen and began washing up, her mind filled with the images of the great snowstorms. Her anger had passed and the voice in her mind was gone, and yet Wyn still felt strange, as if she had done something terrible and had to undo it, but couldn't remember what it was.

Robin came up behind her, asking if she was all right. When Wyn nodded, he picked up a tea towel and started drying the dishes that she'd washed. He began talking in his quick, lilting way, over the sound of running taps and the clink of plates. Robin was just telling her how brave John had been to stand up to his father, when a blackbird landed on the windowsill and tapped on the glass, cocking its head. It came and was gone in a flash, but Wyn was certain that Robin had nodded when the bird had tapped.

When they had put the plates away and had gone through into the sitting room, where Joan was bedding down the fire for the night, Robin announced that he was going outside to bring in more logs. Wyn offered to help, but her foster father was already hurrying into boots and coat. With a wave, he was gone. The log basket remained behind.

A bit later, in the bathroom, Wyn was brushing her teeth while staring out of the window when, to her surprise, she saw Robin making his way uphill. He wasn't carrying a flashlight and was negotiating the slope and the darkness by the faint wisps of moonlight that appeared and disappeared through the snowfall. The scene became more curious when what she was sure was the same blackbird swooped low over his shoulder, landing in a grove of pines further ahead.

The bird nestled in the snowy branches, becoming invisible to Wyn. As she squinted after it, she saw movement from deep within the grove. Someone or something was in there. Wyn remembered the news of wolves on TV and was scared for Robin, but moments later a border collie trotted into the open. The dog and Robin seemed to know each other, the minister giving a wave as the dog bounded forward to greet him.

A bright light shone against the window. Wyn turned to see Lisa, standing in the bathroom doorway holding a flashlight.

"What you looking at?" she said.

"There's a …" began Wyn, before regaining her composure. "None of your business."

"Well? How much longer do you need in our bathroom?"

"I'm not the one who spends hours in here every day," said Wyn. She jammed her toothbrush into a glass and pushed past Lisa. In her bedroom, Wyn drew the curtains and got into bed.

Night was the worst time for Wyn. In the stillness and the silence, an overwhelming sense of emptiness always filled her heart. It had been the same all her life, even after the happiest days with her first foster mother. When darkness came, Wyn felt utterly alone.

Wind was rising and falling all over the house, pushing under doors and through keyholes. Every now and then, Wyn thought she heard the wind whispering a name. She buried herself under her duvet, willing the night away.

3

The next morning, as the radiators were grumbling to life, Wyn put on a dressing gown and padded along the corridor to the bathroom.

She opened the window and leaned out, adding her breath to the morning fog that made the dale seem to stretch forever. For once the jackdaws in the wood were subdued, only squabbling occasionally. Wyn scanned the pine grove, searching for the blackbird and the collie dog from last night. If they were there, she couldn't see them.

Leaving the window open, Wyn ran the bath. When it was full, she turned off the taps and got in. She lay back, listening to the sounds of morning rising across the dale. As Wyn began to drift off, her shoulders dipped under the water, then her neck. And still she sank lower and lower, slipping into a familiar dream.

She was soaring over mountains, her arms flung wide, weaving between warm clouds that hung lazily around the peaks. Winds traveled with her, brushing against her finger-tips. Hidden in the highest mountains, where a pine forest ended, Wyn saw an alpine pass. In the heart of the pass was a small lake, fed by foamy white streams.

Suddenly she was aware of movement in the sky above her. A shadow moved across the sun, casting the pass into darkness. Snow was falling. Ice enclosed the streams. All she could hear was a voice in the wind. Whisper-ing ... whispering ...

Wyn's eyes snapped open.

The mountains were gone. Bath water gleamed gold around her. Her dark red hair swirled above her face. For a moment, Wyn didn't understand. She heard distant bang-ing and the sound of Kate calling her name.

Then Wyn was aware of where she was and she pushed herself upwards. With a gasp, she broke the surface. A wave of water splashed over the bathroom floor. From the other side of the door, Kate was becoming anxious.

"Out in a minute," said Wyn, as she pushed the heavy locks of hair from her eyes and got out of the bath, letting out the plug and wrapping a towel around her. She was reaching for the door, when she glanced in the bathroom mirror. Wyn's hand froze on the latch. Her eyes, normally a dull brown, had changed. Now the brown was nearly obscured by tiny golden flecks. Hurriedly, she rubbed her eyes with her hands and blinked. When she looked in the mirror again her eyes were back to their usual dullness.

"What have you been doing in here?" asked Kate, com-ing into the bathroom and closing the door behind her. "I've been knocking for ages."

Wyn muttered something about washing her hair.

"John called. He wants us to go over to his place and bring a camera," said Kate.

"What does he want with a camera?"

Kate told Wyn, who couldn't believe it.

"I know, that's just what I told him," said Kate, "but he swears it's true. If he's right, we might have a chance of stopping the digging in Skrikes Wood. Unless it's all some complicated plot to get you over to his place? You know, you could go on your own, if you like. Three's a crowd."

"Shut up."

After breakfast, when Lisa was preoccupied on her laptop, Wyn and Kate slipped out into the fog and made their way down the lane.

Pateley Bridge was all gloamy lights. Cars and people moved slowly along the high street. Shadows turned into human beings as they went into shops. At the bottom of the high street, a group had gathered outside the magazine shop. Wyn and Kate peered past them, their eyes widening at the headline of the *Nidderdale Herald*, which was hanging in the shop's window:

WOLVES SEEN IN THE NORTHERN DALES!

"Probably just dogs," said Kate, as they walked out of Pateley Bridge. As they crossed the Nidd, the fog thickened around them.

"Anyway, wolves attack sheep, not people," said Kate. She bit her lip. "Except when there aren't any sheep about. What do they eat when they can't get sheep?"

"Deer?"

"Great. Because Nidderdale is just teeming with deer these days."

A voice called out from behind them. Lisa was walking cautiously through the gloom, her pretty face flushed and scowling.

"Where are you two sneaking off to?" she asked when she caught up with them.

Kate told her what John had said on the telephone. Lisa's scowl deepened.

"He says that there's trees coming into bud in Skrikes Wood? In this weather? This I've got to see."

"Don't you have something better to do?" said Wyn.

"Don't you?"

Wyn had a burning desire to shove the older girl off the road. Lisa clearly read what was in Wyn's mind and stepped back a fraction. Kate was quickly between them.

"I expect an extra pair of eyes won't hurt," she said.

"As if I need your permission," said Lisa, setting off into the fog. When Kate slipped back alongside her, Wyn ignored her friend, angry that Kate had let Lisa join them. She received a light punch on the shoulder.

"Wolf bait, twelve o'clock," whispered Kate, nodding in the direction of her sister.

On a clear day, it was only a fifteen-minute walk to John's house. Today, as the three girls shuffled through the gloom, the short trip seemed to take forever. When Wyn finally stopped glowering at Lisa's back and looked around, she inhaled sharply. Her eyesight had always been good. Eagle-eyes, her first foster mother had nicknamed her, for her ability to pick out a single flower a field away. Now, as Wyn squinted into the fog, she saw layer upon layer of mist fading to nothing. She glanced at Kate and Lisa, wondering if she was imagining things and wasn't reassured to see that they were still inching along, hands reaching out in front of them. Wyn pushed herself to concentrate even harder. Fields appeared and scattered houses beyond them. Soon she could see right up the sides of the dale, all the way to the hilltops.

Wyn snapped her eyes back to the road. Lisa and Kate were still shuffling forward through the fog and Wyn, despite now being able to see far into the distance, did her best to copy their movements. Whatever was happening to her, Wyn prayed that it would stop.

Eventually, they left the road and headed up a long, straight drive lined with snow-caked rhododendron bushes and overhanging trees that lay deathly still in the fog. Wyn could see David Ramsgill's house at the end of the drive.

When they heard the sound of a horse snorting, both Kate and Lisa squinted in the direction the noise had come from. Wyn didn't need to squint. Further up the track, she saw John Ramsgill lead a dun-colored horse across the drive and pause at a gate that led into a paddock. The horse was agitated in the fog, dancing from hoof to hoof, bucking and tugging at its halter. John struggled to open the paddock gate with one hand while also kicking away the snow that had built up at its base. The gate flew open just as John was mid-kick. Wyn saw the boy slip on the snow and fall backwards, losing his grip on the halter and landing right underneath the horse's bucking hooves. Without thinking, Wyn broke into a run. She tore up the long track, grabbing the horse's halter, yanking him away from John. The boy got to his feet and together they calmed the horse before releasing it into the paddock. They watched the animal trot off into the field as if nothing had happened.

"The silly sod," said John. "I thought he was going to trample me to death. He might have done if it wasn't for you."

He smiled at her in a way that made Wyn uncomfortable. She glared at the scrape on John's palm and the bruise that was beginning to show.

"You should put some ice on it," she said.

John scooped up some snow and packed it around his hand, holding it up to show her.

"How's that?"

"You'll live," muttered Wyn.

John was watching her with a thoughtful expression, smiling a little nervously. Kate's voice rang through the fog, calling Wyn's name.

With a quick glance down the track, John began talking hurriedly. "I was thinking we could, if you had nothing on, go see a film in Harrogate some time."

Wyn fixed her eyes on her feet.

"Why?" she said.

"Because, I thought it'd be … I just think we'd have fun. Don't you?"

"There's nothing good on."

"Oh … well … we don't have to see a film. We could do something else. What would you like to do?"

"I'm not really into Harrogate."

The thick fog had hidden Lisa and Kate's approach, but now they were visible near the paddock gate.

"How did you get ahead of us, Wyn?" asked Kate. "And exactly what have we been missing?"

John flushed. He told them he'd be back in a second and ran off to his house. In the meantime, Lisa gave Wyn the filthiest look, then stamped away into the paddock, leaving Wyn to be subjected to a whispered interrogation from Kate. When John reappeared, he had a bandage on his hand and a camera slung around his shoulder. He had also regained his composure, saying enthusiastically to the three girls, "Let's go."

They approached Skrikes Wood along the undulating road from Bewerley. The road had been cleared but not sanded, and the snow underfoot was a hard, white concrete that squeaked beneath their boots.

John was recounting the conversation he'd overheard between his father and one of his men. The man had sworn that trees, which just a few days before were all but dead of canker and cold, had now shed their rotten bark and were coming back to life. Some of them even had buds growing on them.

"My dad told him he'd imagined it, and if he hadn't, to keep it to himself," John told them. "If it had been anyone else, I wouldn't have believed him, but the man used to be a gamekeeper like my dad, so …"

"Which trees?" asked Kate.

"I don't know," said John, biting his lip. "He didn't say."

"So you want us to search the whole wood until we find some trees in bud?" said Kate.

"Yup."

"In the fog."

"Er … yup."

Kate burst out laughing.

"Okay, John-o, but if we find them and get pictures, will your dad stop the digging?"

"I reckon he might," said John, which prompted more laughter from Kate.

"I think it's great what you're doing," said Lisa, casting the full glow of her smile on John, which left the boy even more flustered.

For once, Wyn was too preoccupied to get angry about Lisa's fakeness. Skrikes Wood loomed large and silent ahead, its frozen trees rising up a steep hill. The sight of the wood wrenched at Wyn. Before the snows had come, it had been the loveliest spot in the dale and she had spent many, many happy hours in its scented embrace.

Wyn remembered one expedition with Mrs. March, her first foster mother, pushing through the gate by the river and plunging into a world of dappled sunshine and the heady smell of bracken and wild garlic. The lower parts of the wood were dark and dense with beech, ash and fir trees all clambering skyward to snatch the light. Only a little sunlight splashed onto the river where a family of yellow wagtails bobbed between rocks. Bracken filled the spaces between the trees, with spears of purple foxgloves rising among the green. Halfway up, the giant firs gave way to oaks and birch. Higher still, the wood lightened into delicate silver birches. She and Mrs. March had eaten a picnic on a level grove sitting among the silver birches, watching butterflies and bees drifting up through the wood, searching out light and warmth. Around them, the bracken had been high enough to let the old woman and the young girl view other visitors to the wood unseen. Mrs. March had told Wyn that they were like a little family of nightingales deep in a thicket, hidden from the world, and Wyn had loved being lost with her amongst the green fronds.

Just for a moment, Wyn let herself remember the past. And then the other, bitter memories came for her and she locked them quickly away.

They had reached the rusty metal gate that marked the entrance to Skrikes Wood. John pushed back the gate and they followed him down a path and along a narrow footbridge over the frozen river. On the other side, at John's suggestion, they fanned out and began walking uphill through the deep snow, their heads tilted back as they examined every tree.

While she stared upwards, Wyn had the uncomfortable sense of being watched, and not by friendly eyes. Beeches and oaks, mottled with disease, seemed to tighten around her, hindering her path. Snow clutched at her feet, making each step harder than the last. The others were struggling, too. Kate and John were gasping for air and Lisa had stopped walking altogether.

Her hot temper rising to the challenge, Wyn fought her way on up through the wood, using tree trunks to haul herself onwards. Soon her arms and legs were aching and sweat blinked over her eyes, but she was determined not to be beaten. It was only after struggling on for a few angry minutes that Wyn realized that it wasn't the snow that was holding her up. Every time she put a foot down, the soil under the snow was softening around her boots and gripping onto them. Wyn crouched down and scraped through snow until she reached the dark earth beneath. As she spread her fingers and pushed down into the dirt, she was shocked to feel a faint warmth rising from the ground.

Wyn was so preoccupied that she didn't notice John until he was crouching next to her.

"What's up?" he asked.

"Nothing."

"C'mon, something's up."

Without really meaning to, Wyn found herself telling John, "The ground … it's warm."

He pressed his bandaged hand into the snow beside hers, concentrating hard.

"I don't know. It could be," he said, and Wyn knew that he was lying for her sake.

Now Lisa arrived, with Kate floundering through the snow right behind her.

"What have you found?" said Lisa.

"We thought the ground wasn't so cold around here," said John.

Kate pushed past her sister and crouched next to John, pressing her hand to the soil.

"Feels pretty cold to me … Oh my God!"

Two bees appeared out of the fog, zigzagging low to the snow, heading downhill. They passed right over Kate's hand, causing her to jump up in shock. Wyn watched them go; their brown and yellow bodies colorful against the white ground.

"Bees!" exclaimed Kate. "Real live bees!"

Another pair hurried past. Soon a steady stream of bees was buzzing by. John clicked away with his camera.

"If bees are up and about, summer *must* be on its way!" said Kate.

Wyn saw that the bees were streaming from a knoll not far from where a community of beech and ash trees grew around massive boulders, almost invisible beneath snow. The others couldn't see that far and Wyn didn't dare say she could. Instead, she scrambled up the slope behind the others, following the noisy creatures.

"They're coming out of here," said Kate, examining the base of an old ash. The tree had grown around a boulder, clasping it with its frosty roots. The bees were crawling out of a gap where one of the roots had rotted.

"They must have built their hive in a hollow under the tree," said John, pushing his camera as close to the gap as he could.

They all crouched near the hole, taking turns to peer into it. When it was Wyn's turn, she felt the warmth rising up out of the ground even more strongly than before. She concentrated her gaze, staring down into the hole. Her eyes must have become accustomed to the darkness because she found herself able to see the path the bees were taking down through gaps between the long roots of the ash and the other trees. She saw the bees passing down, down … and for a moment Wyn thought she saw far-off colors and smelled wood smoke. Then it was as if a wall had sprung up in front of her and she couldn't see any further. Wyn redoubled her efforts, trying to glimpse through it. In response, the earth under her shifted so violently that Wyn was knocked away from the ash.

John was helping Wyn to her feet when she saw the old man. He was standing a stone's throw away, in the shadow of two beeches, as lean and mottled with age as the trees themselves. He was dressed like a farmer, in old tweeds with a pack over his shoulder, but Wyn knew all the farmers in the dale and she didn't recognize the man as one of them. To her astonishment, she saw that he wore no boots and his trousers were rolled up to his knees, so that his lower legs and feet were completely bare. His eyes glowed unnaturally green and they were fixed, unblinking, on Wyn.

She was scared, but she had never let herself be intimidated by anyone her whole life and wasn't going to start now.

"What is it?" John asked her.

"Don't you see…?" Wyn broke off, realizing the others couldn't see the strange man.

"See what?" asked John.

"Nothing."

"What are you on about now?" said Lisa.

As the older girl spoke, the collie dog from the night before bounded through the snow, stopping by the old man's side, its hair bristling on its back.

"It's just a dog," said Lisa.

"Looks friendly," said John hesitantly, as he held out the palm of his hand towards the collie. The dog growled.

"Or maybe not," he muttered.

"Top skills, John-o," whispered Kate.

Wyn still couldn't understand why they could see the dog and not the man. He began striding towards them and the dog kept pace, growling at the young people, who automatically began backing away. All except Wyn, until John and Kate grabbed hold of her.

"Whatever happens, don't ..." began John.

The old farmer adjusted his pack and now Wyn saw an ancient-looking axe was strapped to it, its blade wet with snow. Not taking his eyes off Wyn, and still coming towards them, the man drew out his axe.

"Run!" shouted Wyn.

She slapped Kate's hand into John's and shouted for him to hold on to Lisa. Grabbing Kate's free hand, Wyn half ran, half dragged the others in a line, one behind each other, down through the wood. She led them slithering down the bank to the frozen stream, then across the footbridge and through the rusty gate onto the road. When they were all through, Wyn slammed the gate shut and fastened the latch.

Looking up from her task, she saw the old man and his collie dog standing on the bridge, not twenty yards away. He leaned forward on his axe, staring at her intensely. John, Kate and Lisa watched the dog from the road.

"I think we're okay," said John.

"No thanks to you, idiot," Lisa told Wyn. "You never should run from a dog."

"What is that next to the collie?" said Kate.

John was squinting, too.

"There *is* something. It's like a shadow," he said.

Just as he spoke, the man and the collie slipped off the bridge and went back into the wood, vanishing between trees.

"What do you think that was?" asked Kate.

"Nothing," said Wyn.

"It might have been a trick of the fog, like a sort of mirage, because I'm sure there was something," said John.

"You don't believe the freak," said Lisa.

At any other time, Wyn would have thrown back an insult, or worse. For once, though, she had no reply. Against her will, tears were coming. She turned and hurried along the road. Kate called after her, but Wyn broke into a run, losing herself in the fog.

As Kate was calling out to Wyn, the barefoot man reappeared high up in Skrikes Wood, the collie dog at his side. He stood as still as the trees around him, frowning deeply, his green eyes fixed on the girl racing along the icy road, hair streaming behind her.

4

In the crisp early light of the following morning, Kate stood shivering in her pajamas, her arms wrapped around her.

The church bells were ringing for seven o'clock. Behind the house, Kate's horse, Dash, kicked his stable door, wanting fresh air and breakfast.

"I'd better be going," said Wyn.

"Sure you don't want me to come with you?"

If ever Wyn had wanted company on her weekly early-morning task, it was now. All night she had been assaulted by images of the barefoot farmer and all night she had heard the insistent voice of the wind sweeping around the house, whispering a name over and over. She had spent most of the night sitting on the windowsill, peering out into the darkness, desperately trying to think of a rational reason for what was happening to her. Just as dawn had broken, she had convinced herself that it was just her imagination playing tricks on her.

Now, faced with the walk up the dale and the unshakeable feeling that the barefoot farmer was somewhere out there, watching her, her nervousness had returned. The only thing that stopped her from saying yes to Kate was the fear of putting her friend in danger.

"No, I'm fine," she told Kate, as she fastened her snowshoes over her boots. Kate tiptoed outside.

"Don't forget these," she said, handing Wyn a pair of scissors.

"Thanks."

"And keep your eyes peeled for those wolves, Wyn March."

"I'll see you at church," she told Kate, and reluctantly her friend waved her off.

Wyn's path took her across fields from the farm and through the jackdaw wood.

Last night's snowfall glistened on bare branches. The jackdaws' nests were white crowns. The birds treated her as an object of curiosity, heckling her from the treetops. And even though she was sure they were poking fun at her, she was glad of the birds' company. When all the rest of the dale had been cast into silence by the snow, the jackdaws had remained as raucous as ever. To Wyn's mind, they were the tough, beating heart of Nidderdale and her favorite birds.

Leaving the wood, Wyn followed a track onto the Wath road, which carved a line on the hillside above the river. The morning mists were evaporating from the tops. The day was going to be clear; fresh, breezeless. Here and there on the road were the tracks of small animals, which could have been stoats or squirrels — Wyn wasn't certain. They were definitely too small for wolf tracks.

Once she was sure she saw a figure standing stock-still in shadows across the river, but when she stopped and stared, it was only a tree. She was grateful when the road dipped under the cover of ash and hawthorns, and fearful again as the trees thinned and the walls shrank to nothing on the riverside. Wyn heard a rustle behind her and spun around, her heart racing. The road was empty.

On the outskirts of the small hamlet of Wath, she turned up a broad track that led into Spring Wood. As she went up the track, Wyn's fearfulness about the barefoot farmer faded, replaced by an overriding sense of grief. She had made this walk every Sunday for the past three years and it had never become easier.

Steeling herself, Wyn stepped out of the wood. A small house loomed up on the right, half buried by snow drifts. It had been deserted for three years. Other than Wyn, nobody came here anymore.

She forced open the gate, pushing back the week's snow that had banked up on the other side, and stepped into what had once been a front garden bursting with the plants of summer: hotly colored lupins, ruby peonies, and the reds, purples and whites of poppies and sweetpeas.

As she made her way to the walled fruit and vegetable garden behind the house, Wyn remembered all the times she had come back from school in the happy days before her first foster mother's illness. When the weather was good, Mrs. March would almost inevitably be working in this garden. Without looking up, the short, white-haired woman would issue instructions and Wyn would run off to find the things that were needed.

As a newborn baby, Wyn had been found abandoned on the track just outside Mrs. March's house. It had been autumn and Wyn had been left cocooned in a pile of fallen leaves. When nobody had come to claim her, she had been taken in for fostering by Mrs. March. Not that she'd been an easy charge. Wyn had hated being held, screaming every time anyone had tried to pick her up. The local nurse had given up, muttering about the "wildest child there's ever been." Mrs. March had persisted. Weeks passed before Wyn would let the old woman hold her. At nine months, just when Mrs. March was losing hope, the little girl crawled across the sofa and lay against her foster mother. From then on, Wyn relaxed around her foster mother, but only her. When anyone else tried to pick her up, the fiery, people-hating Wyn returned.

As Wyn grew up in the house in the wood, she spent much of her time outside in the garden with Mrs. March. Wyn first crawled, then toddled around the beds of flowers and vegetables, stroking and talking to the plants as if they were her friends. When the garden flourished, bursting with life despite the cooling days, Mrs. March called Wyn her lucky garden charm. She gave the little girl her own trowel and gloves and taught Wyn what she knew, quickly discovering that her foster child seemed to have an inbuilt knowledge that far outstripped her own.

Together they made jam from the fruits in the garden, or rather they picked the fruits together and then Wyn insisted on stirring the mixture on the stove. They went on long walks among the woods and hedgerows to pick sloes and berries. These were mixed with spirits, which Mrs. March refused to let Wyn touch, prompting several heated exchanges.

Even as she grew older, and fractionally more tolerant of trips into Pateley, there was a wildness about Wyn that Mrs. March could never rein in. When thunderstorms rolled across the dale, Mrs. March gave up trying to stop the girl from racing outside and instead would watch her running around the garden, swirling and leaping in the driving rain. Mrs. March also relaxed her rule on Wyn bringing plants into her bedroom, something the girl had done from a very early age, smuggling them inside in her pockets and planting them in drawers and shoes that she had filled with soil.

Fire was a particular battleground, especially Wyn's love of sitting right up against the living-room fire. Any fireguards that were put up would be tugged away when the old lady was out of the room. Every time Wyn was dragged away, struggling and screaming, Mrs. March was sure that the girl must have burned herself, but to her constant amazement, Wyn's skin never seemed to get hot.

Only with the threat of having the fire blocked up and replaced with a fan heater did a glowering Wyn agree to keep a few feet back from the flames. It was a deal that she stuck to occasionally, and only when Mrs. March was in the room.

The greatest struggle Mrs. March faced was over Wyn's hatred of school. There was no convincing the little girl that school might be fun or that she would like being with people her own age. On school mornings, Mrs. March would find Wyn's bed empty and her window open. And even if she did manage to retrieve her foster daughter from any number of hideouts in the wood and take her, kicking and screaming, to school, almost always Mrs. March would get a call from the headmistress to say that Wyn had run off again.

It was Robin Hebden, who taught some mornings at Wyn's school, who would find her. He had infinite patience around the little girl. From a hiding place in the crook of a tree, or one of the old hay barns close to the river, Wyn would watch Robin approach. He would never come directly up to where she was hiding, but would settle down close by and start sketching on a small pad. Eventually, Wyn would come out to see what he was drawing, and how badly he was drawing it. She had soon discovered that Robin was a hopeless draftsman. Trees were lumpen, bushes worse, walls ran across the page at the strangest angles, and when there were still sheep in the fields to draw, they were a cross between dogs and pillowcases. When she came and stood beside him, he would hand her his pad and pencil and let her have a go at sketching the same scene, sighing a little as Wyn drew it with much more skill.

Sometimes Wyn would insist on staying out, or being walked home to her house in the wood. But mostly she would let Robin take her back to school, where she would find a place at the back of the classroom, keeping as far away as possible from other children.

"She won't be shy forever," she once overheard Robin saying to Mrs. March.

"It's my fault. I've kept her hidden away all these years," the old lady had replied.

As much as Wyn and Mrs. March fought, they were completely devoted to one another. For all her independent, indomitable nature by day, Wyn was plagued by nightmares which reduced her to helpless tears. Mrs. March would spend long hours rocking her to sleep, frowning at the way the girl would cry out a strange name with the most inconsolable sense of loss. Mrs. March tried her utmost to stop Wyn's nightmares, but nothing worked, and as the girl grew older, the nightmares only became more intense.

Over time, as the winter snows crept deeper and deeper into the other seasons and the north wind ran over the dale like winter's wolves, Mrs. March began to rely more and more on Wyn. Although her spirit was as tough as hawthorn, the changing weather began to take a toll on the old woman. In the last few years they shared a bed. Mrs. March's presence calmed Wyn when the nightmares came for her, and the remarkable heat of Wyn's body warmed her foster mother through to her bones, so that for a brief time every morning, when Wyn leapt out of bed to make them a breakfast of toast, homemade jam and tea, Mrs March felt back to her old self.

And all the time, Wyn had never felt the cold at all; not once in her entire life. She would think nothing of going outside in just a T-shirt when the hoarfrost glittered on branch and stone. Every time Mrs. March forced a coat onto her, it would end up thrown behind the garden wall.

A blackbird landed on the roof of the house, but flew off almost immediately, creating a little tumble of snow with its passing. Wyn walked through the gate that led to the walled garden, feeling a rush of relief that the flowers she had come to pick were still, miraculously, alive.

They were water avens; lanky, rust-colored flowers, distant cousins of roses. There was nothing remarkable about them, yet they had always been Mrs. March's favorite flowers, appearing in vases and jars all around the old lady's house. While every other tree and flower in the garden was buried under snow, the water avens had survived and bloomed. Wyn snipped some stems from each plant. She left the garden and her old home without a look back, hurrying away towards Pateley and the rising sun.

5

Half an hour later, Wyn was in the graveyard behind Robin's church, wiping snow from a headstone.

She emptied the metal vase of last week's avens and carefully arranged the new flowers, making sure that they were all as upright and outward-facing as possible. When everything was perfect, Wyn took off her coat, laid it on the ground beside the headstone and sat on it, cross-legged. There was still an hour before anyone else would show up. She stroked the headstone, telling the old lady what had happened that week.

The sounds of Pateley grew with the day: a dog barking, the shouts of children, a bus and the sanding truck trying to pass each other on the main street, more cars, and, as always, jackdaws squabbling by the river. There were footsteps. Robin bent down next to her, admiring the bouquet.

"Amazing how the avens are still going. Tough little plants, just like she was."

"Not tough enough," said Wyn, wiping a sleeve across her eyes.

"No, don't be sad, love. She's only gone in a manner of seeing. You and I are here in our boots tramping around in all this muck, but Jane will be flitting here and thereabouts. That's what's lovely about the next life. You can go gadding around like a mayfly on the wind if you like. And when the warm weather comes back and the dale is how it should be, each blade of grass, every wildflower, every leaf on a tree, every ear of corn in the lower dale will be home to a soul that's passed on. At least that's how I like to think of it."

"What if the warm weather doesn't return?"

Robin rested a hand on her shoulder, his breath misting the air around the headstone.

"I believe it will. I believe that God and Nature, who are one and the same as far as I'm concerned, won't give up on us so long as we don't give up on them."

Suddenly, anger surged through Wyn, as fierce as it was inexplicable. She didn't exactly know what she was angry about, only that her entire body was filled with rage.

"Wyn? Are you all right?"

Wyn found herself glaring at Robin, and then felt embarrassed. She fixed her eyes on the ground, until her anger started to fade. She asked her foster father what she could do to help get the church ready for the service.

Together, Wyn and Robin dragged a bag of sand from behind St. Cuthbert's and went to work with shovels. They were scattering the sand on the church steps when big, bluff Brian Davis came striding up. Brian ran the Nidd

Arms pub in Wath, under the watchful eye of his wife Val, and he was Robin's oldest friend in the dale.

"Well, now look at this," he said, admiring Wyn's efforts. "You must come and work for me; show my lazy oafs a thing or two."

"How's the new chef working out?" asked Robin.

Brian let out a long sigh.

"You know, I don't think he's got any taste buds at all. Val's furious, but what can you do? All the good ones head off to the cities these days. Ah, there's Mary."

An old Land Rover pulled up outside the church, with a trailer behind. Robin's older sister, Mary Hebden, got out and her collie dog bounded after her and up the church steps. For a split second Wyn thought it was the same dog from the wood and shrank away from it, scrambling backwards up the steps. Seeing that she was scared, Robin caught a gentle hold of the dog.

"It's all right, it's just old Tess," he told Wyn. "You know she wouldn't harm a fly."

Now that Wyn looked closely at the dog, she saw that while Tess was far older, her muzzle streaked with gray, there was a definite similarity with the collie in the wood,

"She looks just like ..."

"The dog you saw in Skrikes Wood?" asked Robin. Even though Wyn and Kate hadn't wanted to mention what had happened in the wood, Lisa had told her father. And now, was Wyn just imagining it, or were Robin, Brian and Mary Hebden scrutinizing her a bit too closely? After several uncomfortable seconds, they went into St. Cuthbert's, leaving Wyn to continue spreading sand.

She had finished and was sitting on a bench on the pavement outside St. Cuthbert's when she saw John. He sat next to her and took an envelope out of his jacket pocket.

"I've got the Skrikes Wood pictures for Robin."

"Did you show them to your dad?"

"I tried to."

"Well?"

John gave a slow shake of his head.

"Dad wasn't always like this. Before Mum got ill he was talking about selling the quarry and going back to being a gamekeeper. He had this dream of being a head keeper on some big estate and he was going to teach me to track and forage, like Granddad taught him. We had all these amazing plans. But now, after Mum, he spends all his time working and won't teach me anything. He doesn't go for walks much anymore. He's so stubborn."

Not long after his mother had died, John and Wyn had both gone on a school trip to the East Coast port of Whitby. It had been one of the few times that Wyn had left Nidderdale and during the coach journey she had become more and more anxious; both longing to see the sea for the first time and panicking about it. As soon as the coach had stopped, Wyn had run off on her own, ignoring the teacher's calls. She had run through narrow streets, up to the ruined cathedral on the cliff above the town. There she had hidden herself in an alcove among the crumbling stones. Wyn could still remember her whole body shaking as she'd looked down at the endless gray swells. She had watched the fishing boats moving amongst them, the gulls flying beside them. A part of her wanted to run from her hiding place and leap from the cliff, throwing out her arms to soar over the sea, to feel the wind whip her face. She had stayed in the shadows of the cathedral, staring out to sea for hours.

And then John had come, passing so close to where she was crouched that at first she was sure he'd seen her. She had tensed, ready to have a go at him for hunting her down. Instead, the boy had sat in the shade of a crumbling wall and drawn his knees to his chest. Wyn had remained hidden, watching. The boy's unhappiness had struck a chord in her. And years later, when Mrs. March had died and for a while Wyn's world had fallen apart, she had remembered John's grief. At that time, John had gone out of his way to try to talk to her, sometimes walking all the way back to Highdale after school with her and Kate. Even though she'd mostly ignored him, Wyn had appreciated his attention.

The church bells started ringing, sharp and loud through the muffled silence of the dale.

"I'm sorry about your dad," said Wyn.

"Me, too," said John. They sat silently for a short while, watching the morning. John began fidgeting. There was clearly something on his mind. Fearing he was going to ask her out again, Wyn got up.

"I need to help Robin," she said.

"On the bridge the other day, I'm sure I saw something," said John quickly. "But if it was a man, he was so faint, even with the fog and all. I wondered if it might be a ghost. Do you think Skrikes Wood is haunted? We could go back for another look tomorrow."

"There's ice skating tomorrow," said Wyn, glad of the excuse.

"Oh, yes, of course. My chance to finally beat you on a lap around the lake."

"In your dreams," said Wyn, allowing herself a rare smile. John's face lit up.

"Oi! What are you two lovebirds up to?" came a call from the road. Kate was walking up to them, holding a red clipboard. It was a petition demanding that the council abandon the planned digging at Skrikes Wood. When John gave Kate the photographs of bees in the wood, she was exuberant.

"We can hand them around with the petition during collection," she said.

Nervously, John nodded agreement.

That night, Kate crept into Wyn's room and demanded that she get up. There was something important they had to do, Kate insisted.

A short while later, they were outside in the raw night air, leaning over the five-bar gate and looking uphill towards the moor. Kate was shifting her feet against the cold. Wyn copied her friend, shivering when Kate did. There had been another power cut across the dale that evening and the lights hadn't come back on yet, making the quarter moon that had risen over the tops seem very bright. Kate took a silk handkerchief from her dressing-gown pocket. She held it up over her eyes.

"One, two, three, four, five, six …" whispered Kate. "That's six moons I can see through the silk; the real moon and five new moons. That means my true love will show up in five years' time. I'll be a working artist by then. I think he'll be an artist, too."

"Since when are you going to be an artist? What about acting?" said Wyn. All summer she had listened to Kate talk about how she was going to go to drama school and Wyn had responded by picking holes in her friend's plan. She hated the idea of Kate going off and leaving her. Not that she admitted this to Kate.

"I can't help it if I'm multi-talented," said Kate. "Anyhow, my artist lover and I will both become famous and we'll live in a big house in the dale."

Kate held the silk handkerchief up in front of Wyn's face.

"Come on, how many moons?"

"This is stupid. And where did you find this old wives' tale anyway?"

"The Internet. Now, don't be so boring and give it a go."

"Why?"

"John, of course. No, don't frown at me. He really likes you."

"That's his problem."

"You see, I'm not sure I believe you. I think, deep down, you like him, too."

"No I don't."

"Then prove it." Kate pushed the handkerchief into Wyn's hands. "Come on, don't you want to know if there might be anything between you and him?"

Reluctantly, Wyn held up the handkerchief to the night sky and looked through it. A single moon appeared on the other side. She turned the handkerchief this way and that, but the result was still the same; there was only ever one moon. Kate was delighted.

"One? You've got no reflections? That means your true love is here right now. So it's got to be John. Wow, you're in love with John."

"I'm not."

"Are you finally going to let him take you on a date?"

"Shut up."

"He's completely into you. And he's brave. He stood up to his dad today in church, signing the petition right in front of him. You were the first person he looked at after he did it. Don't think I didn't see that. I think you guys will be really sweet together."

"I'm going inside."

Kate crept back into the house with Wyn, chuckling softly down the corridor as Wyn opened the door to her room. "Sweet dreams, Mrs. Ramsgill."

Wyn got into bed and leaned back against her pillow, thinking about John despite herself. He had been brave in church today. When David Ramsgill had seen his son sign the petition, he had gotten up and walked out, followed by several of his workforce and their families. In the whispering aftershock that had spread through the congregation, John had sat alone, his face pale. Wyn could only imagine the reception he would have gotten when he returned home. Kate had offered to go with him, but he had said that he was okay. As Wyn had watched him walk down the hill towards the river, had she felt something for him?

Her thoughts drifted towards the reality of going on a date with John. She'd only got as far as meeting him outside the cinema when something inside her reacted violently against the idea.

Throwing back her duvet, Wyn got out of bed and flung the window open.

What was the matter with her? Why did the merest thought of going on a date with anyone make her feel like this? Determined not to be bullied by her own heart, Wyn put her head under her T-shirt and stared through it, still seeing only a single moon.

"John," she whispered to the night, forcing herself to imagine what it would be like to go out with him.

High up in the night sky, Wyn saw a cloud passing fast across the moon, and suddenly she was filled with the most intense longing. As Wyn stared at the cloud, she felt a fierce will being directed on the dale. It was as if eyes were moving over the rooftops of Pateley Bridge, searching for something or someone. An icy wind whispered through the dale, repeating a name, over and over.

Wyn's hands started to shake. She tried to move back from the window, but her hands wouldn't let go of the sill. They were clinging on tightly, as a strange presence moved ever closer.

Summoning every drop of strength in her body, Wyn prised herself loose from the sill, shut the window and pulled the curtains across it.

A gust of wind blasted against the house, shaking the window so hard that Wyn was sure it would burst open. There was another blast, and a third.

Then, just as suddenly as it had come, the wind vanished.

Thirty miles to the north, at the head of the Yorkshire Dales, there was a pine forest. The trees grew so tight together that they gave no passage to moonlight. The forest floor was as dark as death.

Wolves padded through the trees, the silence of their passing broken by the occasional snarl and flash of teeth.

Four figures walked among them. The man at the head of the group had eyes as green as the lichen that clings to rock. He stopped, glancing upwards.

Seconds later, snow blew from the trees. And now a fifth figure had appeared, a woman with gray eyes and a gray dress that moved with the wind. The green-eyed man took her hand in his and pressed it to his lips.

"What news, Foehn?" he asked her.

"He searches the world. I cannot keep pace with him wherever he goes, but something keeps drawing him to this region. I believe that she is here, Denali."

"We have come a long way for your belief," said a man, as pale as he was lean.

"And we will go further still, Sirmik, so far from our territories that they are nothing but memory," said the green-eyed man. "The end of summer is almost upon us. In just a few days we will be able to save the earth from the destruction that the pair of them have allowed to happen. If there is a chance that she is here, we must find her before he does and stop him from bringing her back from the shadows into power."

"How will we find her?" asked a dark-skinned woman, wearing robes of reds and oranges that matched the fire in her eyes.

"Track down any of my brothers and sisters still living in these valleys and watch them," said Denali. "If this is where she has been reborn, one of them may have become aware of her, and be protecting her. We must divide. Oya, Sirmik, you will search for her in the west."

The dark-skinned woman and pale man eyed each other with dislike. Oya strode away, her robes glittering over the snow. Sirmik followed her. Just as he was leaving the clearing, he glanced back at the final figure, a huge polar bear.

The bear inclined his head. Sirmik walked into the trees. Now Denali faced the bear.

"Kaniq, you head south," he said. "Take my wolves with you."

At once the polar bear broke into a run, shaking the ground as he headed out of the clearing. Where he tore through trees, hoarfrost crackled in their branches.

"I will travel east," said Denali.

"What will you have me do?" asked Foehn.

"What you were doing before. If anyone will guide us to her, it will be him. But be careful," he said.

Foehn's gray eyes gleamed momentarily. Wind blew around her. Then she was gone and Denali was alone in the forest.

6

The next afternoon, with colorful rucksacks bobbing on their backs and golden sunlight glinting off the snow around them, Wyn and Kate trudged downriver beside the Nidd, in the direction of lower Nidderdale. Despite the loveliness of the day and Kate's chatter, Wyn was as jittery as the wind that swept through the dale one moment and vanished the next.

Fifteen minutes out of Pateley, they came to a narrow wooden bridge. It was only wide enough for one and had rails at waist height. Grabbing the rails, Kate crossed the bridge in two swings. When Wyn's hands held the rails, they were shaking. She'd been a mess ever since last night, when the wind had beaten against the house. All night she had been in and out of bed, pacing her room, glaring at the tops of the dale, impatient for the morning to come.

Wyn followed Kate through snow-clad oaks and out to the side of a frozen lake, their shadows cast long in the afternoon sun.

The word had gone out among the seniors of Pateley High to meet for ice skating. There were maybe twenty schoolmates skating and others lacing up their boots on a wooden jetty in front of the disused boathouse. Snowboards, skis and ski poles rested against the boathouse.

Sitting on the jetty, Wyn and Kate took their rucksacks off their backs and got out their ice skates. Wyn was hurrying, fastening the long laces quickly and expertly. She normally hated any activity that involved lots of other people. She'd only gone swimming at the school pool because she knew it was Kate's favorite thing. Skating was Wyn's favorite thing; the feeling of speed, wind, the tangle of bushes and trees at the edge of the lake flashing by. And today, more than ever, she was desperate to get out on the ice and skate off the emotions that were coursing through her. Kate nudged Wyn, glancing at the island in the center of the lake. They both now knew why Lisa had gone on ahead after lunch. She was skating with John, occasionally reaching out to him for support, even though both Wyn and Kate knew that Lisa was a fine skater.

"You've got to be kidding," said Kate. "Look at my sister and your future husband."

Digging the toe of her skate into the ice, Wyn propelled herself forward. She cut a path around the side of the lake, towards the quieter far end. Kate chased after her, and side by side they headed across the ice.

Skating alongside Kate, Wyn felt as though her legs were in shackles.

Only once had Wyn unleashed her true speed on the ice. Just after Mrs. March had bought the red-haired girl her first pair of ice skates, Wyn had slipped out one night, when the moon was newborn and the dale was shrouded in inky darkness, hurrying down through the wood to Gouthwaite Reservoir. Hidden from the world, Wyn had sped from one side of the reservoir to the other, arms flung wide, lost in her familiar dream of soaring over mountains. Only minutes later, unnerved by the acute feeling of being watched, Wyn had hurried home, promising herself that she would never do that again.

Just as Wyn and Kate reached the far end of the lake, they were buffeted by a fierce wind. At the same time, Wyn felt something like an electric shock pass through her. The feeling was so violent and unexpected that she lost her balance and landed painfully on the ice. Dizzily, she got to her hands and knees.

Out of nowhere, a tall boy was sitting down on the jetty. He was leaning over, lacing up a pair of skates, his face hidden by flowing brown hair. Wyn couldn't take her eyes off the boy. Even without seeing his features, there was something incredibly familiar about him. Half of her longed to skate over to him, but the other half wanted to get far away from him as quickly as possible.

The boy pushed back his hair with a gloved hand, revealing an angular face and gray eyes that glittered brighter than the sunlight off the lake. They scanned the other skaters but, to her intense annoyance, never once looked at Wyn.

In one motion, the boy stepped onto the lake and shot away at speed. He moved his legs so effortlessly it was scarcely possible he was able to travel so fast. He scythed through the other skaters, making fast circles around them, spinning to skate backwards, then forwards.

"Are you all right?" said Kate, reaching down and helping Wyn to her feet.

Wyn's throat was too tight to reply. She couldn't take her eyes off the boy.

Turning, Kate followed Wyn's gaze. Her mouth parted to an O.

"Stop the press," Kate murmured. "Who is he? Ever seen him around before?"

"Never," muttered Wyn. But why did she feel so strongly that she knew this stranger?

The boy had shot past the island and was now sweeping towards Wyn and Kate. He leapt up, twirled and landed on one leg with the other leg flung behind him. For the last three hundred yards he didn't move his feet at all, but held out his arms, as if to catch a wind that blew out of nowhere.

Stabbing the tip of a skate into the ice, he came to a stop in front of Wyn.

Slowly, he looked her up and down. When his eyes met hers, there was a look in them that she found impossible to read.

"It's really you," he said.

Wyn's heart was hammering so hard she found herself unable to speak. She was transfixed by his eyes. There was something not quite right about them, but whatever it was, she couldn't put her finger on it.

"Aren't you going to say anything?" the boy asked her.

"Do you two know each other?" said Kate.

Even though Wyn was sure she'd never met the boy before, somehow he was as familiar to her as her own face in
the mirror.

"No," she said.

The boy drew in a deep breath.

"You don't remember me?"

"I don't know what you're talking about."

He stepped towards her, coming so close that she could
feel his breath against her cheek. Despite herself, she looked
back and for a moment she felt like a magnet was drawing
her to the boy. His face was just inches from hers, and moving closer. She thought he was about to kiss her. A part of
her desperately wanted him to kiss her. Suddenly she was
furious with herself and pushed him away, hard.

"What do you think you're doing?" she demanded.

Emotions blew across the boy's face, too quick for Wyn
to follow. Like her, he seemed to be struggling to keep his
composure. Wyn fixed her glare on the middle button of
the military-style jacket the boy was wearing. Kate clenched
Wyn's hand, giving her an incredulous *what on earth* look.

"What's your name?" Kate asked.

The boy turned away from them, staring into the afternoon sky, before replying, "Tawhir."

Wyn frowned at this. Somehow it wasn't the name she'd
been expecting, but when her mind reached for the other
name, it seemed to elude her and disappear.

"Tawhir. Like 'tore here'? What sort of a name is that?"
Kate replied.

Suddenly jealous of Kate and Tawhir having a conversation without her, Wyn glanced up at the boy. It was a

mistake. Immediately he turned back and rested his gray eyes on her.

"What are you calling yourself now?" he asked.

"How can you say you know her, if you don't know her name?" said Kate.

"Names change."

Kate opened her mouth, about to give one of her quick put-downs, when Tawhir smiled at her, the hard lines of his face softening into warmth and humor. Kate's words stuck in her throat. It was obvious to Wyn that the boy was manipulating her friend, but it worked.

Kate was hooked, muttering tamely, "She's Wyn. And I'm Kate."

"You must be Wyn's ... friend?"

Tawhir raised his eyebrows as he asked this.

"Sure," said Kate.

The effect that the boy was having on her friend was driving Wyn crazy. She wanted to grab Kate's hand and drag her away from him, but her body felt like it was encased in ice, unable or unwilling to move. The skating lake, the sweep and calls of the other skaters, the afternoon sun in the trees ... they had become a blur to Wyn. Only the boy remained in focus. She glowered at his coat.

"Wyn," said Tawhir, turning the name over slowly as if he was testing the strength of a strip of metal.

"You're not from around here. Where you from?" said Kate.

"The Alps, mostly. Ever been there?"

"No."

"Your friend has. Don't you remember the mountains, Wyn?"

"I don't know what you're on about. I've never seen mountains, I've never even been abroad," said Wyn, risking another look at Tawhir's face. In her mind's eye, she saw the mountain pass of her dreams.

Just then John skated up, with Lisa in tow. As the two boys stood opposite each other on the ice, Wyn glanced between them. They were both the same age and height, but that was where the similarities ended. While John had the handsome solidity of his father, there was a wildness and endless motion to Tawhir; the way he moved his body in a fluid way, the invisible wind that seemed to blow in his clothes and hair. Only Tawhir's eyes remained still and unblinking. They were now fixed, dangerously, on John. Wyn saw John try to return the stare and then rock slightly back, as if he'd been struck by an invisible hand.

"You okay?" he asked Wyn, touching her sleeve.

A flash of anger passed over Tawhir's face.

"Wyn?" said John.

Wyn realized that she'd been staring at Tawhir for some time.

"I'm fine," she snapped, jerking her head so her hair fell across her face, hiding the unwelcome blush.

"Tawhir here was just saying how he knew Wyn," said Kate.

Both John and Lisa raised their eyebrows at the name *Tawhir*.

"Odd name. You from down south?" said John.

"South, east, north, west … John."

"How do you know my name?"

Tawhir just stared at him.

"What?" asked John.

Wyn was suddenly afraid for John. Even though he was broader than Tawhir, Wyn somehow knew that John wouldn't stand a chance against the tall newcomer.

"Stop it," she said, barging in between them. While John slid back over the ice, Tawhir didn't budge. She had pushed at his chest and her hand was still resting on his coat. It took an effort of will for Wyn to remove it. Satisfaction glittered in Tawhir's eyes.

"Want to skate?" he said.

Wyn was torn — half of her recoiled from his offered hand, the other half longed to grab it. But before she could make up her mind, Tawhir reached out towards Kate.

"Oh, okay," said the blonde girl, before laughing in surprise as the boy grabbed hold of her and swept her away.

"You know him?" asked John.

"No," said Wyn, unable to take her eyes off Tawhir. She hated that he was skating with Kate, not her. And what was Kate doing, going off with him? Across the ice, Wyn saw Kate stumble. Tawhir caught her, keeping his arm around her as they swept on. The sight made Wyn's blood boil.

"Want to race to the island?" said John.

Wyn didn't reply. She took off after Tawhir and Kate, catching up with them as they passed the jetty. Tawhir was skating backwards, pulling Kate along after him.

"Missed me?" he asked.

Tawhir lifted Kate up and spun her in a pirouette,

catching her and lowering her smoothly back onto the ice. Kate burst out laughing.

"Another?" asked Tawhir.

Kate was nodding, but before Tawhir could lift her again, Wyn had grabbed onto her friend's hand. Wyn ground to a halt on the ice, pulling Kate to a stop beside her.

"Ow!" complained Kate, rubbing her arm. Wyn had no intention of apologizing.

Tawhir circled the girls.

"She never used to be the jealous type," said Tawhir, winking at Kate.

"Push off, why don't you?" snapped Wyn. But the boy didn't move and Wyn found that she, too, was rooted to the spot.

"See you, Wyn," said Tawhir. He said her name with a mocking laugh, which made her want to scream.

Tawhir headed off for a corner of the far side of the lake, where the reed beds were thin lances, locked in frost but glittering in the sunshine. Despite herself, Wyn found herself skating after him. Tawhir turned so sharply in front of the reeds that he was at forty-five degrees, his fingertips brushing the ice. Just behind, Wyn shadowed him, following so close in his tracks they were like a train hurtling around a corner.

"Is that all you've got?" said Tawhir, leaping round and skating backwards.

Now Wyn should have easily been able to overtake him, but to her amazement, Tawhir was going faster backwards than forwards. His long hair whipped across his cheeks and not just from the speed at which he was traveling. A hard breeze had come out of nowhere and was blowing around him. Tawhir barely had to put any effort into skating, keeping neck and neck with Wyn, even as she angrily drove herself on faster than ever, gasping from the effort. Tawhir folded his arms across his chest and yawned.

"What are you doing? I know you can go quicker than this."

"You don't know me! You don't know anything about me!"

"I know what your favorite color is. Red."

"Blue," gasped Wyn, lying.

"I know that you prefer dawn to dusk. You love mountains more than deserts, rivers more than lakes."

"No, I don't!"

"Tell me, do you ever dream of flying?"

Wyn was too taken aback to know how to reply. With a yell, she kicked forward, drawing level with Tawhir, who registered her effort with a burst of laughter. He leapt up again, spinning a half circle mid-air, landing on one skate with the other leg stretched behind him. He held out his arms, like a bird. Neck and neck, they went past John and Lisa. Wyn caught a glimpse of their astonished faces.

"What's the boy to you?" said Tawhir as he stared in John's direction.

"None of your business," said Wyn, spotting to her satisfaction the effect that this reply had on Tawhir. As his angular features darkened, he lost a fraction of his pace, and Wyn redoubled her efforts, surging ahead of him for the first time.

She was coming up to the furthest side of the lake, by the reed beds. She swept around the corner, her hand trailing over the reeds that spiked through the ice. Glancing back, she saw that Tawhir had stopped altogether and was watching her. She longed to read his expression, but the boy's long hair had fallen over his face, hiding everything but his eyes.

There were loud cracking noises and suddenly the ice around her was breaking up. Like a dancer, Wyn leapt between the cracks. She had just made it back onto the hard ice when a wind buffeted her and she lost her balance. She was tumbling over the ice, coming to a painful stop amongst the frozen reeds, staring up at the blue sky.

Wyn lay there, catching her breath, half hoping that Tawhir would skate up and lift her to her feet.

The seconds ticked by and the boy didn't come. Furious, Wyn glanced around the lake, searching for him. He was gone.

John, followed by Kate, was skating towards her. Hoping that somewhere out there Tawhir was watching, Wyn let John help her up from the ice.

As the trio skated back to the boathouse, they didn't see the old barefoot farmer watching them from the shadows of trees, close to the lake. His green eyes shifted from Wyn to the skyline, searching for something amongst the high clouds.

The mood at dinner was bad that evening, with Kate, unusually, barely speaking and Lisa clearly enjoying the situation.

And that night, once again, Wyn couldn't sleep. She replayed her encounter with Tawhir over and over in her mind, everything he'd said and every look he had given her. She turned this way and that in bed, threw her pillow on the floor, then retrieved it. She tried to sleep face down, the duvet over her head, which ended up with her pounding her fists against the mattress and leaping out of bed to pace the room.

Several dales to the north, through heavy snowfall, a massive shadow was moving across a moor.

Appearing to smell something, the white bear stopped and lifted his head before breaking into a fast, rolling run, plowing through snow drifts as if they weren't there, heading south, towards Nidderdale.

7

Lisa had been eyeing Wyn from the moment she'd come down to breakfast. But she waited until Kate appeared before launching her attack.

"Seeing your new boyfriend today, are you?" she said.

Outside, the snow had stopped, but heavy clouds remained over the dale, casting everything in a lifeless murk. All the dining-room lights were on and the air smelled strongly of toast. Wyn didn't reply. She was acutely aware that Kate, who would usually leap to her defense, was silent. With a little smile, Lisa continued.

"I've never seen anyone so desperate. You'd only just met him and then you were all over him like a rash, barging Kate out of the way."

"She didn't barge me out of the way," said Kate.

"I saw it with my own eyes. You were having a great time skating with that boy and then she stuck her oar in. And don't tell me you didn't like him."

"He's just some random stranger. And he's gone, anyway. It was like he vanished into thin air."

"What boy was this?" asked Robin.

Lisa told him about Tawhir's appearance at the lake and his mysterious disappearance after Wyn fell over.

"Tawhir ... I've not heard that name before," said Robin. "Where did he say he was from?"

"The Alps," said Kate.

"It's an unusual name for a boy," said Joan. "The only Tawhir I've heard of is a wind in Italy. It blows up the eastern coast, towards the Alps." She glanced sharply at her husband.

"What color were his eyes?" Robin asked.

"His eyes? Why do you want to know?" said Kate.

"Gray," interrupted Wyn.

Robin was holding a mug of tea. He rested it, very carefully, on the table.

"And this boy said he knew you, Wyn?"

"Mistaken identity."

"All the same, I think it would be best if you all stayed away from him in the future. He doesn't sound like the sort of person you want to be mixing with."

"He's probably long gone anyhow," said Kate.

But Wyn knew that Kate was wrong. As soon as she'd woken, Wyn had leapt out of bed and hurried from window to window in the house, and then finally she'd crept outside, half expecting to find him standing in the lane. Even though she hadn't found him, Wyn was sure that Tawhir hadn't left the dale. He was out there, right now, waiting for her.

When breakfast was over, and without staying around to help clear up, Wyn slipped away to the porch. She pulled on boots, grabbed her snowshoes and hurried out into the whiteness. She had only one thing on her mind — to find Tawhir.

Slithering down the icy lane into Pateley Bridge, Wyn was utterly preoccupied with the argument she was going to have with the boy when she tracked him down. Why had he pretended to know her? Why had he pretended to like Kate? And why, after making such a fuss over her, had he run off on her like that, without bothering to see if she was all right after her fall? Lost in her heated thoughts, Wyn paid little heed to the way her senses were nagging at her to get inside, out of the snow. Nor did she hear Kate, until the girl careened past her, out of control on the steep lane. Kate veered into a wall and clung on, composing herself.

"Wyn! Wait up! Where are you off to?"

"I felt like a walk."

"In this weather, and without a coat?"

Wyn hadn't even noticed that she was only wearing a sweater. Kate held out Wyn's parka. They faced each other awkwardly on the shadowy lane. It was Kate who broke the silence.

"I saw six moons."

"What?"

"Outside, last night, I saw six moons. That means that the person I'm meant to be with will be showing up in five years, not now. Besides, it's not me Tawhir likes."

"What do you mean?"

"All the time I was skating with him, he was asking me stuff about you."

"Like what?"

"What you were into, how many friends did you have. If you have a boyfriend ... If that's not a giveaway that he's got a thing for you, I don't know what is."

"What else did he ask?"

"That was it. We kind of got interrupted."

"Sorry," muttered Wyn, not that she really meant it.

"He seemed pretty obsessed. But you say you've never met him before. Honestly? He's not some boy you've had stashed away all these years?"

"No," said Wyn, her heart thumping at the way that Tawhir had been quizzing Kate about her. She tried not to reveal her excitement to Kate, but her best friend was already smiling.

"How many moons did you see, Wyn March? Just one, wasn't it? That means that your soulmate had already shown up, or was just about to. So what if it wasn't John, but Tawhir?"

Wyn shivered involuntarily, hugging her arms around her chest.

"Don't be stupid."

"What's stupid is you and me arguing, especially over a boy. Truce?"

"Truce," said Wyn. She did her best to return Kate's smile, but she couldn't help wishing that her friend would go back to the house and leave her to search for Tawhir

alone. To her irritation, Kate showed no sign of going any-
where.

"Where are you going to try first?" said Kate. "Do you
think he's staying in Pateley?"

"I was going to try the skating lake."

"The skating lake? What would he still be doing there?"

Rationally, Wyn knew that Kate was right. It made no
sense that Tawhir would be out on the lake. But Wyn was
finding that none of her thoughts about Tawhir were very
rational. She just didn't imagine the boy being in Pateley.
People, shops and traffic were just not him. Whenever she
thought of Tawhir, she saw wild, remote places; mountain
peaks, and great, empty oceans.

"I don't know. I just think ..." Wyn's voice trailed away.

"Then that's where we'll look," said Kate. "If you don't
mind company?"

Wyn did mind. All sorts of unpleasant thoughts ran
through her head. What if Kate hadn't been telling the
truth about Tawhir asking all those questions about her?
What if he chose Kate over her again? It took a monumental
effort of will for Wyn to smile back at her friend.

They set off downhill, through the snow. Kate linked
arms with Wyn.

"Let's promise that we'll never let boys ever come between
us. They're not worth it. Yes?" said Kate.

As they walked into Pateley Bridge, Wyn was so distracted
that she ignored the strange way that her bones had begun
to ache and how the hairs were starting to rise at the nape
of her neck. All of Wyn's senses were warning her of some

imminent danger, and on any other day she would have listened to them and gone back to the house. But today Wyn was fixated on only one thing: Tawhir.

"HEY! TAWHIR! HELL-OOO!"

Kate's voice echoed across the frozen lake, becoming lost in the heavy whiteness of the surrounding trees. After peering into the boathouse, she and Wyn had walked across the lake and were now on the edge of the island in the middle.

"TAWHIR!"

"Oh, give up, he's not here," said Wyn. Having built herself up into a fit of nerves, now that the boy wasn't at the lake, she was brimming with anger; even more so because she still had the feeling that he was close by, watching her.

"Shall we go and have a look around Pateley for him?" said Kate.

"No. Let's just go home."

"C'mon, don't be like that," said Kate. "If he's still in the dale, we're going to find him."

"I don't want to find him."

"Yes you do."

"No, I really don't."

Kate hugged her arms to her chest, shivering.

"Am I imagining it, or is it getting colder?" she said.

Wyn found that she was also shivering. Only she wasn't cold. Something was very wrong. She had an overwhelming urge to get off the ice.

"What is it?" said Kate.

Seeing the worry in her friend's face, Wyn looked nervously around.

"Let's get back to Pateley," she told Kate, who nodded agreement.

Then Wyn saw him.

There was a faint, crackling noise all around them. All over the lake, an icy crust was forming over the newly fallen snow. Wyn and Kate watched, breathless, as hoarfrost swept over the surrounding trees; trunks and branches crackling in the transformation. A pair of jackdaws rose up into the sky, departing noisily to the south.

The barefooted farmer, his axe held in front of him in two huge hands, was striding out of the trees behind the boathouse.

8

In the days and nights since she'd last seen him, Wyn had steeled herself for this moment. Whoever or whatever the barefoot farmer was, she'd promised herself that if she ever saw him again, she'd hold her ground.

Now, as the man stepped onto the ice, his collie dog at his side, Wyn fought the fear that was shaking through her bones and drew herself up as tall as she could. She locked eyes with the approaching farmer, and at once felt the force of his will. For a moment Wyn imagined that she was trying to face down all the oaks around the skating lake. The effort made her head hurt. She buckled a little, but didn't break her stare.

Kate's hand reached for hers, squeezing tight.

"Oh my God, what is that next to the dog? Is it a ghost?" said Kate.

"You see him now?"

"I don't know what I'm seeing. What are you seeing?"

"I don't know."

Suddenly, the man's green eyes gleamed, as if a light were shining through them. Kate jumped.

"Oh my God, I can see him … oh my God."

Kate tugged at Wyn's hand, but Wyn was stubbornly determined not to retreat. The barefoot farmer broke into a loping run, far faster than his age would suggest.

"Come on!" gasped Kate.

Without breaking pace, the farmer was raising his axe over his head.

"Wyn!"

Wyn found herself almost being yanked off her feet by Kate. The girls turned, slipping and slithering away from the running man, when in a spray of snow, a huge white bear appeared on the other side of the lake. Bounding over the reed beds, the creature thundered across the ice towards them. Caught between the farmer and the bear, the girls froze, not knowing what to do.

"Get off the ice!" yelled the barefoot farmer, running past them, green eyes blazing, the collie dog at his side.

He met the bear head-on, swinging his axe at the creature. A great paw swatted the axe away and then the bear was on top of the man, clawing at him and snapping at his neck. Wyn was sure that the barefoot farmer was going to be killed, but he had taken the bear's paws in both hands and, incredibly, was pushing the huge creature off him.

The bear was twice his size and many times heavier, but Wyn saw that somehow the man was a match for him. Even though his feet slipped on the ice and the creature wrestled to free his paws, the man kept forcing the bear away.

Then the bear stopped struggling. His eyes, colorless as the ice of the lake, gleamed with a pale light. Opening his mouth, the bear breathed long and hard on the man.

A glittering mist seeped over the old farmer. Wyn saw frost form on his face and hands and all over his worn tweed clothes. Angrily, the man kept pushing the bear back over the ice, but as the frost gripped him, each step became harder. The bear was wresting his paws from the old farmer's grip. Slowly, his fingers were being unlocked. With a crackling of frost, the man inched his head towards Wyn and Kate.

"Run," he rasped.

Then the bear's paws broke free and the farmer was sent tumbling from a single blow to the head. He lay, unmoving, on the ice. The collie dog leapt between him and the bear, snarling for all it was worth. The bear raised a paw and was about to strike the dog, when he stopped, sniffed the air, and fixed his eyes on Wyn and Kate.

The creature began padding towards them.

Kate leapt for the farmer's axe. She began swinging it over her head, her whole body rocking from the weight of her weapon.

"Get back!" she yelled at the approaching bear.

In reply, the bear struck the surface of the lake with a paw. A split second later, ice rose up from the surface around Kate and Wyn, fastening itself around their legs and creeping up their bodies. In a split second, Kate was frozen rigid. The axe fell from her hands. To her horror, Wyn saw ice going into her friend's mouth and covering her eyes, dulling the blue in them until they were almost colorless. Wyn tried to walk to her friend, but the ice held her tight. She felt it latching itself to her face and pulling at her hair.

Rage exploded in Wyn. With a yell she tore first one foot, then the other, free from the frozen lake. As she stepped towards Kate, all the ice fell away from Wyn, landing in shards on the lake.

Wyn was too concerned about her friend to notice a golden light that briefly illuminated the falling ice.

The bear was all teeth and claws, ice and fury. Roaring, he reared up on his hind legs, dwarfing the two girls.

Hugging Kate close to her, Wyn waited for the creature to crush them.

Winds billowed all around the lake, stripping snow from the trees. Out of nowhere, Tawhir appeared next to Wyn, his arms flung wide.

Now the gale drove into the bear, rippling his white coat. He dropped to all fours, snarling.

Her arms still locked around Kate, Wyn watched Tawhir, awestruck. Incredible as it seemed, Wyn knew that Tawhir was making the wind. He stood on the ice, long hair whipping over his face, his eyes filled with the same unnatural light as the barefoot farmer and the bear.

With a roar that showed every inch of his huge mouth, the bear bent his head into the gale and took a step forward. Tawhir fell to one knee, his head bowed, arms stretched straight in front as if he was trying to stop a train. The bear kept coming. Now he was only a few yards from the boy.

"Wyn," gasped Tawhir, as the bear took another pace closer. "You're stronger than him, drive him off."

Wyn had no idea what Tawhir was talking about. She couldn't do anything but stare, uncomprehending, at the boy and the bear. The bear was taking another step closer, his teeth snapping inches from the boy's hands. Tawhir took a step back. The bear roared with satisfaction, his pale eyes burning bright.

"Quickly. Use your fire!" gasped Tawhir, glancing back at Wyn.

"My what?!"

"Your fire! Now!" Tawhir was shouting.

"Fire?! What fire?!" she yelled back, holding onto Kate and shaking her head at the boy, who had turned his attention from the bear and was staring at her in disbelief.

The old farmer was rising to his feet behind the bear, raising his axe. At the last second, the creature spun around. The old farmer's eyes blazed with a green light that also washed over his arms, running down his axe. The blade slammed into the bear, lodging itself deep in the creature's chest. As the bear tried to tear out the blade, the man sprang forward and seized the bear by the neck, forcing his hands into the creature's fur as his eyes blazed and sweat ran down his face. They faced each other for a moment; man and bear. Then there was a crack and the bear was falling, his head lolling, and meanwhile the green light was fading from around the barefoot man.

The wind vanished. Other than the sound of the old farmer's heavy breathing, the skating lake was silent.

As the old farmer wrenched the axe from the bear, the creature disintegrated into glittering flakes of snow.

Leaving Wyn's side, Tawhir walked to the bear's remains,

moving the finger of one hand in a circular motion and whispering something under his breath. A small tornado, no higher than the boy, gathered up the snow lying on the frozen lake and spun it upwards into the sky and then northwards.

But Wyn only watched the tornado for a moment. She was rubbing off the ice that had formed on her friend's face and neck and gently picking it from her lips. Kate's breath was coming in a whisper, so faint that Wyn was terrified it would stop at any moment.

The barefoot farmer crouched down beside her, reaching for Kate.

"Give her to me," he said.

"Keep away," cried Wyn, hugging her friend close.

The old man gave an exclamation of impatience. "I'll not hurt Robin's little girl."

To Wyn's surprise, she found that she knew his name: Thwaite.

"Quickly now," he insisted.

Reluctantly, she let him take Kate. He cradled her against his chest, holding her with one of his huge hands. With the other, he slipped his canvas pack from his shoulders and laid it on the ice. Taking a large earthenware pot from the pack, he opened it and scooped out a handful of purple paste, which he gently rubbed into Kate's forehead. The paste sparkled when he touched it and, to Wyn's relief, a little of Kate's usual color returned. Taking her face in his hands, Thwaite called Kate's name, telling her to wake. She didn't stir. Frowning, the man repeated his words. Wyn's previous hope turned to panic.

"What is it? Can you help her?" she asked.

"Not here, not on the ice."

Telling Tawhir to bring his axe and pack, Thwaite lifted up Kate and strode off across the lake.

"Where are you taking her?" demanded Wyn, hurrying beside the barefoot farmer, who was heading towards the bank in a long, loping gait. His collie dog trotted beside her. In answer, as soon as they were off the frozen lake, Thwaite bent down and shoved aside the snow. When it was cleared, he laid Kate down with infinite care and knelt beside her, placing both his hands on the exposed ground. Wyn watched Thwaite push his hands into the hard soil. He shut his eyes, breathing deeply.

For a moment, nothing happened. Wyn stood dead still, arms gripped around her chest, sick with worry for her friend.

The same green glow that Wyn had seen on Thwaite's arms when he struck the bear now formed on the earth under his hands. It crept up over his fingers and spread across his whole body. The ground trembled. All around the lake, Wyn heard the trees creak and saw branches sway even though there was no wind. Sweat broke out on the farmer's face. His breathing grew fast and deep.

It's a dream, Wyn thought. None of this is real. She wasn't outside, on the ice. She was asleep in bed and Kate was asleep in her room across the corridor.

Wyn almost jumped out of her skin when Tawhir appeared right in front of her. Throwing down the axe and canvas pack, he shook Thwaite's shoulder.

"Are you insane, earther? You don't have the strength for this. Let Wyn get the ice out of her."

"What can she do?" said the old farmer, his hands still pressed against the ground and his chest heaving with strain.

"Anything! Everything! How blind *are* you? You must see who she is."

"I know exactly who she is. She's Wyn March."

"She's Mugasa."

The old farmer glanced at Tawhir, then Wyn, in utter disbelief.

"You've been flying too close to the moon and it's muddled your mind. Mugasa died. We all know this. The child has the gift and that's all."

"Who do you think the bear was hunting?" insisted Tawhir. "And why was she untouched by his cold? Yes, Mugasa died, but she was reborn. Wyn *is* Mugasa."

The old farmer fixed his eyes on Wyn, shaking his head as he looked her up and down.

"Impossible," he muttered.

"Stop bothering with me and look after Kate," snapped Wyn, hating the attention. But even as she was speaking, Wyn saw that Kate's face was turning a deathly white again.

Snatching his hands from the ground, Thwaite clasped Kate tight to his chest. The muscles in his face and veins on his hands stood out. Wyn almost fell over as the ground trembled. As before, the trees swayed around the lake, but more violently this time, shaking snow from creaking branches. Sweat was pouring down Thwaite's face now and his breaths were coming in gasps. The shaking that had begun in his arms now spread across his entire body. Slowly, the green light seeped out of his eyes, and as it did, the ground and the trees fell silent.

Struggling to keep control of himself, Thwaite laid Kate back on the exposed earth.

Then he was beset by rasping coughs. He leant back on his haunches, gasping for air. The collie dog padded over to Thwaite, pressing close to the old man and watching him anxiously.

Wyn dropped to the ground beside her best friend. Kate's eyes were still shut, her expression unchanged. Wyn took off her coat and laid it over Kate. She did this as gently as she could, terrified in case the weight of the coat extinguished completely the last sign of life in her friend.

9

Supporting himself with his axe, Thwaite pulled himself to his feet. He put his fingers to his lips and whistled a short, lyrical burst of music.

Moments later three blackbirds — a male, a female and a younger female — swooped through the snow-clad trees and landed on Thwaite's outstretched palms. Without saying anything, he looked closely at the birds, brushing his fingers and thumbs against their wings and tail feathers. Thwaite cast the blackbirds back into the air. Wyn watched them fly fast and low, towards Pateley Bridge.

With the greatest care, Thwaite lifted Kate into his arms and began striding after the birds.

"They'll find Robin and bring him to the outskirts of Pateley. He can take Kate to your doctors. Perhaps they'll be able to help her," he told Wyn, who had to jog alongside him to keep up. The collie dog bounded ahead.

They passed under the trees at the edge of the lake and scrambled down onto a twisty track beside the river that Wyn had never seen before. Wyn was too preoccupied with Kate to notice the trees shifting around them, their branches moving to let them through. One of Kate's hands hung by Thwaite's waist and Wyn clasped it, praying and hoping that the doctors would find a way to help her friend. To Wyn, the continuing argument between Tawhir and Thwaite was like noise in a far-off place.

"Doctors?!" exclaimed Tawhir, who was effortlessly keeping pace with them, passing over the snow without making a sound. "Will you listen to yourself? You know that there's no human doctor who can draw the ice out of that girl. Wyn's the only chance she has."

"It's time you were moving on, boy."

"Cold doesn't touch her. She's got no parents. She was born at the very moment that Mugasa died, when the world started to turn colder. Ring any bells?"

"Coincidence."

"At least test her. You can do that, can't you?"

"I've work to be getting on with and no time for distractions."

"Of all the blinkered, stubborn earthers, you take the prize!" exclaimed Tawhir. "The end of summer is in three days! Three days until the last chance to restore balance to the world is gone! And now, by a miracle, we've found her — the supreme spirit — the one being who can turn back the snows and you won't even test her. Why? Let me guess. Is it because you're afraid that you might look a bit stupid for not spotting her for all these years? Better to keep your pride intact than grasp the last chance we have to save the world from an everlasting winter."

The old man's face darkened.

"You think I haven't watched this girl from the moment she came to my dale? But she is a girl, a human child. Mugasa would never have been reborn in this form."

"Of all spirits, you know better than any of us that we do not choose the form of our rebirth," said Tawhir, blocking her path. Now his face was inches from Wyn's, making her feel disorientated and angry and giddy all at once.

"Get out of my way," she said.

"Not until you start telling the truth. We know that cold doesn't touch you, but what other powers do you have that you are hiding from us? What about water and wind? Can you bend them to your will? And fire?" Tawhir took a slow breath. "What power do you have over fire?"

A shiver ran through Wyn. She felt like the boy, with his piercing eyes, was dragging all her fears into the light. Furiously, she shoved him away from her.

"Shut up! Just shut up!" she cried. "Kate's hurt and you're going on about some crazy rubbish. I don't know what you're talking about and I don't care. If you can't do anything to help Kate, I just want you to go!"

Tawhir had been rocked back by her hands. He recovered his balance and took a step towards her.

"Do as she says," said Thwaite.

Tawhir's features hardened into a cold mask, and for a split second Wyn was sure that she'd seen that same expression on him, but in a different time and a different landscape. There was something so familiar about him. The boy raised one hand, and Wyn thought he was going to lash out at Thwaite. She saw the barefoot man brace himself and reach over his shoulder for his axe. Tawhir's hand dropped to his side. Wind and snow whirled around him until, with a last glance at Wyn, he vanished. A small tornado was climbing fast into the murky sky. Narrowing her eyes, Wyn saw the tornado had a shadow inside it.

Snow had dusted Kate's face and hair. Slipping off her sweater, Wyn used it to carefully wipe the snow away.

"Who are you people?" she demanded, turning back to Thwaite.

The old man didn't reply. He was watching her, frowning.

It took Wyn a moment to figure out what he was staring at. Without her sweater, she was only wearing a T-shirt, and she had forgotten to shiver. Self-conscious under Thwaite's scrutiny, she hastily put the sweater back on, muttering what Mrs. March used to tell her when she was little. "I've got good circulation."

Two of Thwaite's blackbirds returned, chattering noisily. On the path above, Wyn heard Robin calling out. Shouting a reply, Wyn scrambled out from the tunnel under the trees and up the bank. Thwaite came behind her, carrying Kate, and Robin was running over the snow towards them.

The rest of the day was a nightmare for Wyn: hurrying alongside Robin as he carried Kate to the Pateley Bridge Medical Center; a frantic Joan and Lisa appearing; the car journey behind the ambulance to Harrogate; and then the squeak of the hospital floor as Wyn wandered alone, around and around Harrogate Hospital, praying that Kate would be all right; watching her friend through a window, lying in bed, the doctors unable to bring her out of her coma; Joan not looking at Wyn as she sat at her daughter's bed; Robin driving her and Lisa home; a dinner that nobody had any appetite for; Lisa going on and on at her, refusing to believe that Kate had simply slipped on the ice and hit her head.

In the end, Wyn ran upstairs to her room. She sat with her back to her bedroom door, her face hidden in her knees, replaying in her mind the moment when Kate threw herself between Wyn and the bear. However much she tried to hide from it, in her heart, Wyn knew that Tawhir was right. She was the one that the creature was interested in.

It was almost a relief when the power went off and Wyn's room was plunged into darkness.

10

She was still sitting on her bedroom floor when, hours later, the house cold and silent and snow drifting past the windows, Robin tapped lightly on the door.

Wyn clambered painfully to her feet, stiff all over, and let him in. Wyn's first question was about Kate. The vicar shook his head. He looked as exhausted as Wyn felt.

"I spoke to Joan and she says Kate is comfortable. The doctors have done more tests and we should have some results in the morning. These things always take time."

Wyn returned to her place on the floor, drawing up her knees in her hands.

"It should have been me in hospital, not Kate. She wouldn't have been at the lake if it wasn't for me. And when the bear ... she was the one who tried to fight him off. I panicked. I didn't do anything to help her."

"What could you have done, love? I've seen Thwaite lift fallen trees and move boulders the size of a car. If he couldn't stop the bear, then I don't imagine anyone could."

"It still should have been me."

Robin sat on the floor next to her, and for a while they both watched the snow falling.

"Who is Thwaite?" asked Wyn.

"He's been safeguarding the dale since long before any people settled here. Every tree, every plant, every flower and every animal in the dale is under his stewardship."

"Like a sort of farmer?"

"I've always thought of him as a gardener. Nidderdale is his garden and he tends it. He's a spirit of nature, a guardian of the earth. I'm not an expert in these things, but I do know that he's not alone. There are many other spirits of nature like him all over the world, hidden from sight. Some, like Thwaite, look after the earth, others guard the waters, there are spirits of the winds, and spirits who bring fire and others …"

Electricity surged through Wyn's body and a second later the window blasted open, snow billowing into the room. Robin went to shut it, then gave a gasp of surprise. Out of nowhere, Tawhir had materialized on the windowsill. He dropped lightly into the room.

"… who watch over the cold places. Ice spirits, such as the bear," said Tawhir, finishing Robin's sentence.

He was walking around the room and inspecting it with an expression of faint amusement.

"And if Wyn had exerted herself just one little bit, the bear would have been running northwards as fast as he could and your daughter would be sleeping soundly across the corridor.

"I've been talking with the old earther on your behalf. One of the more unpleasant few hours of my life. They've got no people skills, earthers. You try cheering him up with a lot of warm air about his sorry little territory — how charming it must be in spring and, oh, what a lovely knoll of sycamores — and what do you get? A thank you? A bunch of flowers? No, a load of abuse and an axe swinging at your head. It took forever, and a lot of promises from me —"

As Tawhir bent to examine a glass box of bangles on Wyn's chest of drawers, his hair fell down across his face. Like an invisible hand, a breeze blew the hair back from his eyes. Wyn felt Robin's intake of breath.

"A wind spirit," Robin murmured.

"... Finally the old stuck-in-mud has come to his senses," continued Tawhir. "He wants to see you now."

"What for?" asked Robin.

"To test her."

"What do you mean *test her*? What's all this about?" said Robin.

Tawhir's eyes were locked on Wyn's. She glared back at him.

"Don't you want your friend to get better?" he said. "There's not a doctor in the world who can heal her, but you can. You could melt the ice in her in an instant. You have gifts, Wyn, gifts that you've kept hidden for too long. You can choose to keep them locked away. If you do that, your friend will never recover. She will lie in hospital for the rest of her life, never waking. Or you can unlock your true power and become who you were born to be. You won't just have the power to save your friend. You will be able to change the face of this frozen world."

Tawhir hopped onto the window frame and held out his hand.

"Thwaite is in his wood, waiting for you. I can carry you to him."

While Wyn longed to take the boy's hand, a warning voice inside her made her shrink from him. A strange expression passed over the boy's face. He turned from her, his long hair masking his features.

"Don't be late. He's not the waiting type."

The boy leapt into the night. Wind blew behind him, banging the window. Wyn went to fasten it, expecting to see him running over the pale fields. There was no sign of him and no footprints on the freshly fallen snow around the house. Beside her, Robin nodded up into the night sky, a trace of wonder in his tired features.

"All my life, I've wanted to see a wind spirit. I never thought I actually would," said Robin. Wyn could see how hard he was trying not to look at her differently. "Do you know what he was talking about, love?"

Wyn took a deep breath, summoning up the courage to tell him what she had never revealed to anyone else: how she never felt the cold, how she could sit inches from a roaring fire and never get burned, and how it was as if Tawhir had stepped out of the deepest corner of Wyn's mind. In the end, all she could manage to share with Robin was a shrug.

"You don't have to go," he told her, and despite herself, Wyn was desperate to stay. But she saw the hope in Robin's eyes and knew what she had to do — for him, for her friend.

"I want to," she insisted.

Tears filled Robin's eyes. He took her hand, squeezing it. "Then we'll go together," he said

As quietly as they could, so as not to wake Lisa, Wyn and Robin crept out of the house and set out for Skrikes Wood. In the dale below, Pateley Bridge lay motionless, wreathed in streetlamps and snowfall. At the bottom of the lane, jackdaws were savaging a pile of garbage bags.

"I was a boy, some years younger than you, when I first saw Thwaite," said Robin. "Mary and I were walking by Gouthwaite Reservoir one winter's morning, looking for some sheep that our father was missing. Brian Davis had come up from Wath to help us. We were quite a threesome back then, always getting into trouble. Not unlike you, Kate and John."

Robin described how a strange farmer had appeared out of nowhere.

"He was perfectly normal-looking, until we noticed that his legs were bare below the knee. He stopped, looked at us and then walked under some hawthorns and vanished from sight. We ran after him, but he was gone. Now, Mary and I knew every farmer in the dale and didn't recognize him. Besides, who'd ever heard of a farmer going about barefoot? We weren't sure if we'd seen a madman or a ghost. All we did know was that we had to find him again."

Robin told how after weeks of looking for the barefoot farmer all around Gouthwaite Reservoir, the three of them had been coming over the bridge at the bottom of Pateley one evening and to their surprise found Thwaite waiting for them on the other side.

"I think he wanted to ambush us since we'd been trying to ambush him," said Robin. "There were people walking right past him, but we were the only ones who saw him. We had the gift, he told us later."

"What's that?"

"Some people are able to see the spirits. Don't ask me how or why. All I know is that it's a gift from nature and we were lucky to be given it, and luckier still to be open to it. Not everyone who is born with the gift sees the spirits. Thwaite told me once that there's others in the dale who have the gift but have turned their backs on nature and never learned to use it. If only they knew what they were missing. The things Mary, Brian and I have seen when we've been helping Thwaite and his lover around the dale."

"His lover?"

"A water spirit called Naia. She is, or was, the guardian of all the rivers and streams in the dale. But don't mention her in front of Thwaite. She's another one the ice has taken."

Robin fell silent and now Wyn grew increasingly panicky at the prospect of the tests that Thwaite had in store for her and the meaning of Tawhir's words: "Change the face of this frozen world."

11

The iron gate at the entrance to Skrikes Wood slammed in the darkness. Thwaite came striding through the deep snow, his collie dog bounding beside him.

"How's young Kate?" he asked.

Robin gave a shake of his head. The collie padded forward and pressed itself against the vicar.

"Hello, Pip," said Robin, stroking the dog.

Thwaite signaled Wyn to come close. Trying not to show her fear, she did as she was told. As she took those few steps, the night seemed to close around the wood. Clouds were thickening in the night sky. She had the acute sensation that Tawhir was nearby, watching her every movement.

"Give me your hands," said Thwaite.

"What for?"

Without asking, Thwaite took Wyn's hands and pressed them, palms down, to the cold bough of one of the beeches.

"Can you feel anything?"

"It's rotten. And wet," said Wyn, her relief tempered by a mild disappointment. So, was that it?

"I'm not talking about the outside. Still your mind and concentrate. Now, can you feel its heart and its soul?"

Shaking Thwaite's hands off, she rubbed her palms against the bark, digging her fingers into its ridges. Once again, there was nothing. She shook her head.

"You're certain?"

"It's a tree," snapped Wyn, frustrated at failing a test that she didn't understand.

Thwaite gave a long exhale of breath and turned his attention away from Wyn.

"That's that, then. Robin, you'd best take her home."

Wind whipped around her and a second later Tawhir was there, flushed with anger.

"Try something else," he demanded.

"I've wasted enough time on your fantasies and now I've better things to be getting on with."

"Like watching yourself getting buried by snow? She *is* Mugasa. You've got to test her again."

As Thwaite and Tawhir argued over her, Robin put his arm around her, whispering, "Let's go home, love."

In a blur, Tawhir was in front of Wyn, blocking her way.

"I've seen you do this so many times before. There was a forest, high in the Alps. You used to go there and spend hours in the company of trees. Don't you remember?"

And for a split second, Wyn found herself breathing in the hot, rich scent of fir trees and saw familiar snow-capped peaks gleaming through branches. She recognized them as the mountains of her dreams. Tawhir was watching her intently.

"You do remember, don't you? I can see it in your eyes."

"I've never been abroad," Wyn whispered. And she never had. Mrs. March would barely leave the dale, and the freezing weather had put a stop to the Hebdens' travel plans.

"Don't you want to help your friend, Mugasa?" the boy demanded.

"Stop calling me that!"

"Why? It's your name."

"My name's Wyn!" she yelled, slapping her hand against a beech in frustration.

Immediately, she felt something like a low electricity; a faint trembling in the heart of the tree. She pressed both hands against the bough. The electricity surged. Startled, she pulled her hands away with a cry.

"What *is* that?" she said.

"What? What did you feel?" asked Tawhir.

The boy was thrust quickly out of the way by Thwaite and now Wyn found herself looking into his intense green eyes.

"Tell me what just happened?"

When Wyn told him, the old man grew very still.

"Do it again, just don't upset him this time," said Thwaite.

"Him?"

"The tree, who else? He's a good one for conversation, but like all beeches he's proud and easily offended. So I'd start with saying sorry if I were you."

She was aware that Tawhir and Robin, too, were watching her every move. Disconcerted by their stares, Wyn closed her eyes and cautiously laid her hands on the tree.

At her touch, the tree vibrated hard, almost like an upset swarm of bees. Wyn found herself whispering an apology, which would have been the strangest thing she'd ever done if the tree hadn't responded to her. Its vibrations lessened and then, to Wyn's amazement, silent images began flashing in her mind: rain falling hard in the wood, dripping off the green-clad branches of the nearby trees; a rabbit digging just where the farmer had rested his axe. She saw the surrounding trees as saplings, no higher than the bluebells that encircled them. The tree gave a funny quiver and the next thing she saw made her gasp. It was herself and Mrs. March. She would only have been one or two, toddling around with a mushroom in her hand and snatching at a toadstool on the ground, before being pulled away and bursting into a temper. The image was gone as fast as it came, replaced by snow falling on a gray evening.

Wyn's heart had leapt at the sight of her old foster mother and now she was frantic to get that image back. She squeezed the bough, begging the tree, "Show me that again." But the tree wouldn't repeat it, however much Wyn pleaded.

She became aware of Thwaite resting a hand on the bough above hers.

"Make it show me that again," she demanded.

"No. They aren't to be forced," said Thwaite. His voice was tight with tension.

"What's going on?" asked Robin.

"They're showing her their memories," said Thwaite.

"That's more than just the gift, isn't it?"

"It may be," said Thwaite.

The earth spirit led Wyn from tree to tree, telling her to lay her hands on them and speak out what she saw. Oak, beech, fir, lime, holly; some trembled so hard her hands shook, others barely quivered, but they were all eager to share their memories with her.

No one memory was the same. One beech remembered a sunset through the high branches, while a lime tree a few feet away showed Wyn snapshots of a hundred years of springtime snowdrops, vibrating with pleasure in the years when the white flowers rose up around its trunk with an unbroken perfection. A fir tree showed her mistle thrushes eating red berries from a rowan across the fields. The trees never lingered on the snow and frost that now left them stripped and pocked with decay. They preferred to show Wyn memories of warmer days. But as much as Wyn clambered through the thick snow to touch bough after bough, each time whispering a fervent plea to the trees, she never saw herself with her foster mother again.

A thick-limbed oak deep in the wood showed her Thwaite towering down, his giant fingers feeling the trunk. For a moment Wyn didn't understand, then she saw saplings behind him no higher than his knee and realized the tree was showing her when the wood was first planted. Water droplets sparkled on a cobweb strung between two saplings. All around, the wood was wet with dew and the misty light of dawn. Thwaite was scooping up dew from the wood floor and washing his face with it. Thwaite was much younger then, his hair straw-colored, his eyes glossy as new grass. He was smiling. Beside him, Wyn saw a young blue-eyed woman walking barefoot through the damp wood. She put an arm around Thwaite, stroking the back of his neck. The image passed and the tree showed her acorns blowing against broad leaves.

Thwaite prised her hand from the trunk of the oak.

"That's enough," he said.

"You believe me now?" Tawhir asked Thwaite. The boy was practically hopping from foot to foot with excitement. She found herself wanting to smile back at him but caught herself just in time.

"I don't know," muttered Thwaite.

"How much more evidence do you need?" asked Tawhir. "She's not an earther, but she's got your powers and more besides. Who else could she be?"

"What is all this about? Who do you think Wyn is?" said Robin.

"The best thing you can do is to go home and forget what you've seen," Tawhir told the priest. "Don't tell anyone and don't come back here. Anything you do to draw attention to us or Wyn will only put her in danger."

"What sort of danger? What's all this about, Thwaite?"

"The boy here thinks Wyn is one of us."

"Wyn's a spirit?" said Robin breathlessly, and as he spoke Wyn felt her stomach turn. She reached for her foster father's hand, conscious of Tawhir watching her intently.

"It's time you went home," said the wind spirit.

As the boy spoke, a stiff breeze picked up around Robin, jostling and buffeting him. Wyn clung to Robin, yelling at Tawhir to stop.

A huge hand grabbed Tawhir by the scruff of the neck and threw him to one side. The boy vanished before he hit a tree and reappeared, rubbing his neck and glowering at Thwaite. All around Wyn and Robin, snow drifted silently to the ground.

"You're in my territory, which means you'll behave yourself," said Thwaite, which brought an angry interjection from Tawhir. The old man muttered under his breath and all at once the ground underneath them shook and Tawhir was cursing as he was sucked downwards, as if he'd just stepped into quicksand. He stopped sinking when the snow was up to his waist, but continued to struggle and complain.

"One more sound out of you and you'll be getting an up-close look at beech roots," said Thwaite.

"Of all the lousy, stinking earthers ..." said Tawhir, only falling silent when he had been dragged down to his chin.

Thwaite went down on one knee in front of Wyn, looking deep into her eyes.

"Do you know how you can communicate with the trees?"

"No," said Wyn.

"And you have no memories of a past life? None whatsoever?"

Wyn's heart was pounding and her mouth had turned dry. Was this the meaning behind the strange dreams she'd had since her earliest years? Often Robin had talked in sermons about the cycle of life, death and rebirth — much to the annoyance of some of his parishioners — and his words had always unsettled Wyn. But the idea that they could actually be true, and that Wyn had lived before and remembered that life in her dreams ...

"I don't know," she whispered.

"Of course you do," said Tawhir, spitting out snow as he spoke.

"Oh, hold your noise," said Thwaite, and the boy was sucked down further, protesting furiously. Face, hair and finally shaking fists vanished. There was a muffled sound underground and then silence. The earth spirit returned his attention to Wyn. While his face was as lean as winter, his green eyes still held a little of the youth of spring, a last act of defiance against the cold.

"We've had no summer this year," Thwaite told Wyn. "There's been no thaw and none coming. In just three days, this moon will be gone and summer will be over, not just for this year but for who knows how many years to come. A terrible ice age will descend upon the world and all its living beauty will die. But I believe there is one supreme spirit who has the power to bring back summer.

"Her death heralded the start of the cold weather. Many of my kind believed that she had been reborn somewhere in the world and would return to us one day. But as the years passed and the snows crept into spring and then turned our summers white, still she didn't come back. Some of my kind lost all hope. But a few of us, like Tawhir, kept searching for her. It was an impossible task, like looking for a single blade of grass in all the fields of the dale."

Wyn's head spun. She felt sick and faint all at once. Unable to bear Thwaite's searching eyes, she concentrated on the snow at her feet.

"You think Wyn is this missing ... spirit?" she heard Robin ask.

"I don't know what to think. Since she was first found in the dale, I've kept my eye on her. Until now she's shown almost nothing more than a little skill in Jane March's garden. It's hard to believe that the one we are looking for would, or could, keep her true powers hidden for all these years. And harder to believe that she would have returned in human form. The boy, on the other hand, says he knew Wyn in her old life and is convinced it's her."

Wyn's mind raced. Was that why Tawhir felt so familiar to her? Whenever she had dreamt of the valley in the mountains, Wyn had always had the feeling that there was someone else there with her, like a shadow by her side. And yet, in all her dreams, she'd never seen the face of this other person. Was it Tawhir? Even though she was sure that she had known him before, something about the boy and the shadow didn't match up.

Wyn forced herself to look up from the white ground.

"What do you want from me?" she whispered.

"What do you want from yourself? That's the true question. None of us know how Mugasa died. And if you truly are her reincarnation there's a reason that you have stayed hidden from us for so long. In my meadows I have flowers that leap up one year and then don't show themselves for decades. I've tried my best to figure out why, and I still can't come up with a good answer. It's not wind or rain, sunshine or the pull of the moon; it's not cold winters, short summers or a change in the earth. No, they wake when their hearts tell them to. For three thousand summers I've watched over all the living things of this dale, but I've never been master of their hearts, and I would not try to be the master of yours. This is your decision, Wyn. Only you know if it's time to wake."

"What about Kate? If I was this missing person, would I be able to make her better?"

Thwaite rose to his feet and retrieved his pack and axe.

"If you are who the boy thinks you are, you will have the power to change the world."

With a word to his dog, the barefoot man strode off uphill, into the shadows. Wyn listened to his footsteps and the crashing noise Pip was making as she bunny-hopped after him through the deep snow. She wrapped her arms around herself, feeling her heart pounding in her chest.

"Listen to me, love," said Robin. "Forget about everything else, even Kate. What is your heart telling you?"

In answer, anger surged within Wyn. A fierce anger and a voice that told her to defy all of them and stay hidden. The voice was like her own, but amplified a hundred-fold and so powerful that Wyn rocked on her feet and might have fallen back into the snow had Robin not reached out to steady her.

At his touch, the voice receded and Wyn's heart once again reached out for Kate and Tawhir. But even as it did, the echo of that great voice lingered within Wyn, warning her of something. Though what it was, she didn't understand.

"What is it, Wyn?" Robin was asking.

"Nothing. I'm fine. I want to go with him."

"Are you sure?"

Again the voice rose up in warning, and again Wyn ignored it, nodding to Robin.

Her foster father took her hand, then called out to Thwaite. The old man stopped and waited while Robin and Wyn trudged up to him.

"Now you take good care of her," said Robin. "And if anything happens to her, anything at all, you'll have me to answer to."

"Go home, son," said Thwaite, reaching forward and briefly squeezing Robin's shoulder.

"Come back to us the second you want to," Robin told her. But as he said it, Wyn saw the sadness in his eyes and had the same feeling that she'd experienced the last time she'd said goodbye to Mrs. March in hospital. She stood awkwardly, wanting to hug the priest, but unable to. There were tears in his eyes when he leaned forward and kissed her on the forehead.

He gave her a warm smile and Wyn forced a smile back. Then Robin was gone, walking downhill through the trees in his quick, jerky way.

The iron gate clanged shut in the distance.

Thwaite led Wyn to the large ash, whose roots had grown around a large boulder. It was the same tree she'd crouched beside with Kate, Lisa and John a few days ago when they had watched the bees.

He was about to lay his hand on it, when he bent down and scooped up a handful of snow. Amongst the glittering white flakes were the brown and yellow stripes of a bee. Carefully Thwaite blew away the snow from the tiny creature's wings. With his free hand he delved into his pocket and brought out a small jar and prised off the lid. A pungent smell of honey filled the air. Thwaite dabbed in a finger and offered it to the bee. It stirred, drowsy, then set to work on the honey, crawling over Thwaite's finger until he shook it off into the roots of the ash.

"And not so far, next time," he called after it, before stroking the trunk of the tree.

Wyn watched in amazement as, with a lot of creaking and cracking, the roots of the tree pushed the boulder out and to one side, just like a door opening. Taking the collie and his axe in one arm, Thwaite went backwards into the opening.

"Well, come on now," he said to Wyn, before disappearing from sight.

Wyn watched Pip's eyes looking up at her, as man and dog swayed their way downwards on a ladder of roots and twined brambles. Warm air rose up from the hole, carrying a rich fragrance of flowers.

Wyn lowered herself onto the ladder. When she was a few rungs down, the ash creaked as it drew the boulder back into its roots. Wyn scarcely noticed. She climbed down into the earth, her eyes widening at the extraordinary scene that lay beneath her.

12

Wyn had left winter and climbed down into summer.

The air was deliciously warm and wet, full of the scent of flowers and wood smoke. Jumping off the last rung of the ladder into long grass, Wyn turned slowly around, scarcely believing what lay before her.

She was standing in a meadow in an enormous cavern, at least fifty feet high and so huge that it must have stretched the whole length of the wood above. Water was dripping from the roots of trees that dangled down from the cavern roof. At the edge of the meadow, a bonfire crackled brightly. She saw other bonfires further off. The dripping water and the fire smoke filled the cavern with a murky haze.

Before, in the wood, everything Thwaite and Tawhir had been saying had felt a little unreal to Wyn. They had been talking about a world that she had only ever glimpsed in dreams. Now she felt that those dreams had been made real. The color and beauty of this place rippled through her body, making her want to shout out with delight.

A little way ahead, Thwaite was surrounded by chattering birds that mobbed the air around him before landing, sometimes three at a time, on his hand. He looked at each one intently. The birds responded with bobbing heads, chirps and sharp bursts of song.

Muffled yells and movement caused Wyn to look up. A pair of thrashing legs was dangling from the cavern roof. She recognized the black jeans and pointed leather shoes.

"Is he all right?" Wyn asked.

"Wind spirits will do anything for attention. He can get out whenever he wants," said Thwaite. His words brought more furious kicking.

"What is this place?"

"See for yourself," replied Thwaite, returning his attention to the birds in his hands.

Wyn wandered away from him, peering and inspecting. Many of the wildflowers that had lined the track up to Mrs. March's house were there: the whites of stitchwort and cow parsley that used to make the old woman sneeze and the hot pinks of red campion and foxgloves, tall and forbidding.

One meadow led into another; a purple expanse of betony and knapweed that narrowed into a path between brambles and willow herb. Pushing through the path, Wyn stepped out into a glade of rowan and cherry trees, her ears full of the roar of bees. All the bees in Nidderdale must be down here, Wyn thought, as she skirted around the edge of the trees. Wyn saw what looked like giant eggs made of straw, leaves and twigs hanging amongst the upper branches of the trees. At the bottom of each egg, the straw fanned out into a small opening. Bees streamed in and out of these openings and Wyn realized that they must be beehives, but unlike any she had ever seen.

Squirrels were clambering over many of the hives, joined frequently by birds carrying twigs and plant stalks. Wyn watched, astonished, as the birds deposited their loads beside the squirrels, who would then set to work weaving the fresh materials into the hives. All across the glade squirrels were hard at work, some repairing hives, others weaving them from scratch and all the time being supplied by convoys of blue tits, linnets, goldfinches and numerous other small birds Wyn hadn't seen in the dale since last year.

But as she watched all the animals, Wyn began to notice that there was something very wrong about this strange, subterranean summer. The birds flew too fast, the bees jostled each other on flower heads and there was panic in the leap and hurry of the squirrels. The excitement that Wyn had first felt when she'd looked around the cavern was quickly leaching away, replaced by a deep sadness. This place was an illusion of summer and the animals knew it, however hard they tried to fool themselves. With a heavy heart, she made her way back to Thwaite.

He was waiting for Wyn in a meadow on the far side of the glade. He was sitting amongst trefoil, watching a pair of blue butterflies dancing from side to side over the yellow flowers, dodging the water that dripped continually down from the roof of the cavern.

"Did you do all this?" asked Wyn.

"Most of it. The animals helped, of course. There's every type of plant, bush and tree that grows in the dale down here. They wouldn't have survived another winter up top, so I made the cavern and filled it as best I could. It'll protect them, for a little longer."

"How much longer?"

"Perhaps a year. Two for the strongest. But this is no home for living things. They need sun on their faces and wind in their bones. Every day I'm losing some and they're not coming back. And there's nothing I can do to stop it. There'll be other earth spirits with caverns like this who will keep things going on a little longer. But sooner or later, if this winter holds, even the greatest of my kind will bow to the inevitable."

"How many like you are there?"

"What did Robin tell you?"

"Just that you and the other spirits looked after nature."

Thwaite led her out of the meadow, into a circle of silver birches, underplanted with a deep blue carpet of veronica. The embers of a small fire glowed in the heart of the circle, with a pile of rotten wood beside it. He picked up a branch, turning it in his huge hands.

"In the early days of the world, there were no spirits. Left to their own devices the forces of nature were wild, unbridled. Chaos reigned. To bring some order to the chaos, the earth created the spirits. They were created as guardians of nature, each with responsibility over individual elemental forces: wind, fire, ice, water and earth, which it is my task to protect.

"We live for a long time, but are not immortal. When our lives are ending, the earth brings forward a new spirit to take over from us. The young spirit is trained by the old, who then dies.

"You ask how many of us there are. Once there were many of us. I can remember when there was a water and earth spirit for every dale. But these past centuries, few new spirits are being born. Old spirits are dying and their territories are no longer guarded. Now there are just a handful of earth spirits still living in the dales. All the water spirits are gone. Some left, and those that chose to remain have been taken by the ice. Neither dead, nor reborn."

Thwaite's eyes dropped to the branch in his hands. He threw it onto the fire. The flames wrapped themselves around the rotten wood. Smoke streamed upwards.

"What happened?" asked Wyn.

In a tantrum of wind that shook the birch trees around them, Tawhir thumped down among the veronicas.

"Have you told her who she is yet?"

"I'm coming to that."

"Any time you're ready ..."

Thwaite threw out a hand to grab the boy, but Tawhir was too quick, retreating into the branches of a silver birch. His eyes were fixed on Wyn. She felt herself flushing, but before she could say anything, Tawhir disappeared again. Thwaite continued his narrative as if nothing had happened.

"The spirits were created to protect and rein in their elements. But among us there have always been those who have sought to expand their territories. For the most part these conflicts were small. A fire spirit might fight with an earth spirit and run wild in his territory, or some tussle could take place in the sky between a water and a wind spirit. But occasionally things would get out of hand and groups of spirits would gather in great numbers to wage war with each other, destroying whole territories with earthquakes, hurricanes, floods, fire and ice.

"So once again, the earth intervened. To keep the peace and protect the balance of nature, the earth created two supreme spirits, giving each of them power over all the elements. They can control the oceans and summon earthquakes, hurricanes, fire and snow. These two beings can take any form they like, but in their true form they are what you humans call dragons."

"Dragons!" exclaimed Wyn. "Real-life dragons! You've got to be joking! They're myths, fairy tales!"

But as she spoke an image flashed through Wyn's mind. She saw clouds rushing past her and the wide ocean curving away far below. She shook her head clear and was back in the cavern with Thwaite watching her.

"The two dragons are the earth's champions. For thousands of years, they have kept the peace and helped nurture life on earth. They themselves are opposites. There is the ice dragon, Sh'en Shiekar. His power grows in the winter's cold. And his partner is Mugasa, the fire dragon, whose strength lies in the heat of summer. Their great power is matched only by their secrecy. In all my years tending this dale, I've never caught sight of them, or known another spirit who has."

"Why do they hide, if they're so powerful?" said Wyn.

"They're not untouchable," said Thwaite. "For all their strength, they can be killed, and there have always been spirits who have resented being governed by the dragons. In recent times, that resentment has turned to anger and rebellion. It was the rise of humans that changed everything. The early humans knew of the spirits and worshipped them, but over time humans began to change the face of the world, causing great damage to nature. Many spirits turned their power against humans, but the dragons did not.

"A rebellion took shape. There were secret gatherings, alliances formed between spirits who once fought against each other. Their one goal was to find the dragons and kill them. Then, unfettered, the spirits would be free to turn their fury on humans. I don't know how it happened, and I would never have believed that such a thing would have been possible, but somehow the rebels slipped through the defenses of Mugasa, the fire dragon, and killed her.

"It was an act as reckless as it was ill-conceived. They have put the earth in the greatest danger of all. Without Mugasa's fire to balance Sh'en Shiekar's ice, the world has grown colder and colder. Without a summer this year, the world will slip into an endless ice age and all living things will die."

The earth spirit's green eyes were fixed unblinking on her. Wyn began backing away from Thwaite, her stomach turning.

"No, it can't be me ..."

"Why not?"

"Are you serious? You're telling me that I'm a dragon? A real-life dragon!"

"There are just three days left until the end of summer," said Thwaite. "Time enough for you to discover your old power and bring warmth back to the world."

"Let me get this right. You're saying I've got three days to become a dragon and save the world?" said Wyn.

"I will do my best to train you. I'll help you to remember," said Thwaite.

From the tree, Tawhir was slowly nodding. And all at once Wyn was filled with anger; anger at Thwaite, at the things he was saying, and above all at Tawhir. And in amongst her rage, a great wild voice filled Wyn's head, telling her over and over to get away from the two spirits. She began backing away from them.

"Find someone else to put this on," she muttered.

Then she was running. She tore across meadows and through trees and bushes, throwing up her hands as branches whipped at her face. She reached the vine ladder that she'd climbed down earlier and was scrambling up it when it shook with a gust of wind and Tawhir appeared, hovering next to her.

"Where are you going?"

"Get away from me!"

"The earther is right. You're the only hope for the world."

Wyn was nearly at the top of the ladder. The roots of the other trees dangled down around her, and with them came the smell of the cold night. She pushed at the stone blocking the entrance to the cavern. It didn't budge. Consumed with her blind panic to get out of the cavern as fast as she could, Wyn slammed her hand into the stone, yelling, "Come on!"

With a painful crackling of roots, the stone was drawn back. Tawhir came between her and the entrance.

"You think that ice spirit was alone? Right now every rebel spirit is searching for you, many of them far more powerful than the bear. If one of them catches you in the open, there's nothing Thwaite and I will be able to do to protect you. Your only chance is to stay hidden with us and to try to unlock your old powers. If not for yourself, what about your friend? You're the only one who can save her."

Wyn wanted to push past Tawhir and reached out a hand to shove him out of the way, but just as she was about to touch his chest, her hand stopped of its own accord. It held there, shaking.

Tawhir vanished.

Wyn scrambled through the entrance and out into the starlit wood.

Behind her, the stone was noisily drawn back into the roots of the ash. Wyn stumbled among the trees, breathing hard, as her head slowly began to clear. She was expecting the boy to reappear beside her at any second. But he didn't come.

The silence of the night grew around her. Snow began to fall, thick and fast, casting a veil over the moon, turning the distant lights of Pateley to haze. She clung to the trunk of a holly, the tips of its glossy leaves dipped in ice.

Wyn felt the tree vibrate under her hand. Beneath her feet, she sensed the warmth of the cavern and the last vestige of summer that clung there. Her thoughts were full of Tawhir. She forced them away. Now she saw Kate, lying in the hospital, her once ruddy face lost in the white of winter, just as Mrs. March's had been.

There was a noise close by. Thwaite was climbing out from the roots of the ash, Pip under his arm. Fighting down the warning voice inside her, Wyn let go of the holly and trudged uphill to where the earth spirit was standing. It took all her willpower to find the words.

"All right," she whispered. "Test me, train me, I'll do whatever you want me to do. I don't know what I can do, if anything, but I'll try."

Snow was gathering on his coat. He stood there, tall and lean, stroking Pip's head with one of his great hands.

"That's as good a place to start as any. Now we'd best get on our way."

"Where to?" Wyn asked as they left the wood. Instead of taking the road, Thwaite climbed a stone wall and dropped down on the other side.

"My home," he said.

13

Wyn had walked through Nidderdale all her life, but she had never seen the paths that Thwaite led her along that night.

They went on secret ways that hugged close to stone walls and hedges and that ran in the shadows of trees. Paths appeared in impenetrable bramble thickets. As they neared Pateley Bridge and Wath, tunnels opened for them in the riverbank. Although Wyn walked in darkness, to her eyes these roads through the earth were clear as day. Then they were stepping out onto the shores of Gouthwaite Reservoir, snow blowing hard over its icy surface.

Every so often the path alongside the reservoir vanished under snow drifts the height of stone walls. Thwaite plowed through the deep powder, carving a way for Pip and Wyn. The earth spirit was breathing hard, but his pace never slowed. Often he glanced over his shoulder, scanning the landscape behind them, then drove on harder still. Wyn didn't notice when Thwaite finally stopped. She crashed into the back of the earth spirit.

"We're here," he said.

They were standing in front of three sprawling hawthorn trees that lay a stone's throw from the ice and were surrounded by a mass of snow and brambles. The hawthorns were growing so close together their branches interlocked. Cobwebs stretched across the few gaps in the branches, billowing in the wind. The whole effect was of a giant, rotting spider's nest.

A long, drawn-out howl came from far off through the darkness. Wyn had never heard anything quite like it. It was too bleak to be a dog, and, despite herself, Wyn shivered at the sound. She saw again the huge white bear rising up above her, teeth and claws bared.

"Wolves. I've not heard them here for three hundred winters," said Thwaite, squinting uphill towards Fountain's Earth Moor. Wyn picked out dark shapes, heads low to the snow, moving just below the skyline.

Pip was fretting, baring her teeth in the direction of the wolves.

"Don't be so daft," said Thwaite, catching the collie by the scruff and leading her to a gap in the brambles where two hawthorn branches hung down, forming a sort of archway. Thwaite shoved Pip through the gap. The collie disappeared, crashing through the unmistakeable sound of leaves.

"You, too," he told Wyn.

From beyond the archway, Wyn caught the scent of flowers and heard Pip's soft cough. She ran her hand around the archway, and, as she did, white blossom and green leaves materialized, hanging down like curtains. Drawing them apart, Wyn stepped forward into Thwaite's home.

The wind and snow vanished and she was walking over a deep carpet of white and purple thyme flowers into a living space that was every bit as unexpected as the cavern had been. It was the size of a small barn, but far more comfortable and colorful than any barn Wyn had seen. Two large chairs, with deep cushions of sheep's wool and leaves, were set by a stone hearth and beyond them a kitchen table with two plain chairs and a massive dresser. Above the table and dresser, the hawthorn branches interlaced and stretched to form a sleeping platform with a window on the left-hand side. Small stout branches growing out of one of the three trunks formed a ladder up to the platform, which was even more thickly padded than the fireside chairs. The second trunk formed a pillar at the entrance Wyn had just come through and the third grew up through the dresser.

Green hawthorn leaves dotted with white blossoms formed the walls and roof. Amongst the walls were windows, glazed with what Wyn thought was old glass, until on closer inspection she saw the panes weren't glass at all, but translucent cobwebs. The weather outside pushed against the fine strands but couldn't get in. As she traced her fingers over the windows, spiders came clambering over the cobwebs inspecting the places Wyn had been touching.

The young female blackbird landed on the windowsill and began hopping towards the spiders, its beak slowly opening. Thwaite shooed it off.

"How many times do I have to tell you. Yes, you! And don't pretend that you were just going to pass the time of day!"

He hung his pack on the green and white wall opposite the hearth, where rows of branches jutted out like coat
hooks. Hanging from the other branches were a vast array
of gardening tools: spades, forks, mattocks, hoes and many,
many more. As well worn as many of them looked, their
handles gleamed with polish and their blades were razor
sharp. Below all these tools and all along the side wall was a
massive earthenware cauldron, scrubbed clean, and scores
of burlap sacks, full to the brim with dried wildflowers.

Wyn felt that she had walked into part home, part
garden-shed and part tree-house. While Thwaite knelt by
the hearth, rubbing sticks of kindling together, she took
off her boots and padded around like a cat, inspecting
every inch of her new environment. With each footstep,
the thyme carpet gave off a deep scent of musk.

She quickly discovered that Thwaite was fastidiously
well organized. From the cauldrons and sacks that were
laid out in neat lines under the gleaming tools, to the perfectly stacked dishes on the dresser, to the rows of preserve
bottles above the dishes, each sealed with a square of cloth
and tied in a precise bow; there was a rigid discipline to
Thwaite's house, despite the fact that it was built of leaf,
bark, bramble and cobweb.

Wyn quietly opened the drawers of the dresser, her heart
quickening when she saw what they contained. They were
full of small animals; mice, frogs, snakes and hedgehogs, all
fast asleep in beds of sheep's wool.

Pip was shaking the snow out of her coat in front of the
hearth. Wyn went over to the collie and examined the intri-
cate carving on the backs and arms of the two chairs. One

showed images of the fields and woods of the dale, rich with the flora and fauna of spring. Carved into the other chair were the running waters of the Nidd, widening and narrowing; trout-fast then minnow-slow.

Thwaite had got the fire going and laid on logs, watching them as they caught. Using a flaming splint, he lit several lanterns that were suspended over the table. With the lanterns and the fire burning, his home became even lovelier in Wyn's eyes. Thwaite told her to take a seat by the fire and asked her if she was hungry. She nodded eagerly. While Thwaite went to the dresser, Wyn watched the flames in the hearth, listening to their soft voices. In the past, when she had thought she'd heard whispering from the fire at Robin's house, Wyn had put it down to a trick of the wind or her imagination.

And now ... what if she really was the reborn fire dragon?

Checking that Thwaite wasn't looking, Wyn sent her thought towards the fire.

All at once she felt the flames sense her, just as the trees had done. Excitedly, they reached out to her, whispering urgently. Wyn was filled with a surge of energy so wild that she thought it would burst free of her body. The flames leapt up in the hearth, illuminating the room. But just as she felt that she was losing control of herself, all her instincts raged against the fire, warning her to stop what she was doing.

She wrested her thought away from the flames and they dropped back just as Thwaite turned around, frowning from Wyn to the fire. She clung to the sides of the chair, doing her best to mask her emotions. The flames *had* reacted to her. Even though she was doing her utmost to ignore them, the flames were whispering out into the room that they were ready to obey her, that she just needed to call on them.

Outside, a wolf howled, followed shortly by a deeper, answering howl. Thwaite went over to the cobweb window. "The pack has split up. Half of them are keeping to the tops. I can't tell where the others are. They're hunting something, that's for certain."

"Hunting what?"

"Whatever it is, it's not an animal, not at this time of night."

"You think they're after…?" Wyn was about to say *me* and caught herself. She got out of her chair and stood next to Thwaite, following his gaze. Even through the snow and darkness, Wyn could pick out low shapes bounding over the distant moors. She blinked, wondering if she was imagining it. But, no, when she looked again the shapes were still there and this time even clearer. She saw the outline of ears and long muzzles. Involuntarily, she took a step back from the window.

Thwaite picked up the water jug and drenched the fire. The flames hissed, calling out to Wyn before fading to smoke and nothingness. She felt a flash of anger towards the earth spirit.

"They may well be after you," he said. "And unless they were servants of the bear, it means that they are doing the bidding of another spirit. It could be an ice spirit. We'd best hope it's not one of my kin."

"An earth spirit?"

"I have heard of earth spirits who keep wolves as familiars, but none with territories in Europe. More than other spirits, we draw our strength from the territories we tend.

The further we travel from where the earth created us, the weaker we grow. If the wolves obey an earth spirit, it must be one of unusual power."

Thwaite returned to the window, his huge hands gripping the stone sill.

"There are two earth spirits in nearby dales who could help us. Hackfall and Old Mal. They're strong, Old Mal most of all. If only I could be sure they were on our side."

"You think they could have joined the rebels?"

"They've long been my friends, but how can I be sure of what lies in their hearts? This rebellion has divided and poisoned the spirit world. No, until you return to your true self, we trust no one."

"How do I know I can trust you?"

"What sort of fool question is that? Of course you can trust me," said the earth spirit. "The boy is another matter. My bones tell me that there's something not right about him. He claims that he knew Mugasa, but why would she reveal herself to a low-ranking wind spirit? No, he's not telling us all of the truth."

Wyn didn't like the sense she had that Thwaite was right about Tawhir. The wind spirit *was* holding something back; she was sure of it. Nevertheless, her heart jumped as she felt Tawhir's presence coming suddenly towards them. The hawthorn shook violently as he landed in the room. White petals fell around the wind spirit and for a split second Wyn had a vision of him surrounded by snow.

14

⬧⬧⬧⬧

Tawhir began emptying the contents of his pockets and laying them in a line in front of the hearth.

"Chips, peanuts, cookies and … in my view the high-point of human endeavor … chocolate."

Wyn watched Tawhir produce nine bars of chocolate, then stop and mutter to himself before finding one more tucked into his sock. After a brief contemplation of his pile, he offered Thwaite a Bounty. The earth spirit glared back at him.

"Not a Bounty fan?" said Tawhir, sifting through the pile before reluctantly holding out the Toblerone. "But only because you're putting me up for the night."

"And when did I agree to do that?"

"I've been over every inch of your territory and all the others surrounding it. If there were other spirits out there, I would have seen them."

"What of the wolves?"

"Heading back north, with a stiff wind to hurry them on their way."

"A stiff wind? What sort of foolishness have you been up to?"

"Relax, earther, they weren't aware of me."

"If that's true, you can go back out there and follow them, find out if they were acting alone."

"Since when did I become your lackey? The wolves are gone and there are no other spirits bearing down on your little territory. But there might be if I spend all night going back and forth over the dales. The wolves won't notice me, but there are other spirits out there who could. Then they might ask themselves, what's a wind spirit from southern Europe doing so far to the north? Is he looking for someone? Has he found someone? If you want to go out and advertise that we've found Mugasa, just two days before the end of summer, then that's your business. I think I'd rather keep under cover tonight. So if you'd like to break a habit of a lifetime and start showing some hospitality, a bed wouldn't come amiss."

Thwaite pointed to the floor.

"And I want you out and keeping watch by dawn."

"That's the gratitude I get for saving both your lives today!" exclaimed Tawhir.

Thwaite pointed to a chair, and in reply Tawhir pointed to the sleeping platform. He winked at Wyn.

"There's room up there for both of us."

"I'd sooner sleep on the floor," said Wyn.

Pushing past them, Thwaite laid his hand on the hawthorn whose branches formed the sleeping platform. He bent his head, talking softly. With a sound of creaking and rustling of leaves, branches of the hawthorn tree stretched down, interweaving tightly and sprouting new leaves and blossom, until there was a solid wall down the middle of the platform.

"You can have the view," said Tawhir, vanishing and reappearing on the windowless side of the platform. Wyn felt a rush of panic.

"Go on up and get some rest," said Thwaite, as Wyn hesitated at the ladder. Her hands were trembling. She gripped the ladder as hard as she could to make them stop. "Tomorrow will be a long day for you."

"What's going to happen?"

"A miracle, I hope."

Wyn clambered up to her side of the platform. Once there, the green wall was reassuringly dense and some of the panic she was feeling lessened. The platform was surprisingly comfortable with its mattress of wool blankets and springy branches, and she quickly discovered that she wasn't alone. As she inspected her bed, she came across other lodgers: a family of weasels curled up together and a whole pile of snails next to a wall. In amongst the hawthorn branches above, she saw thrushes and fieldfares and, eyelids half-open, a row of tawny owls.

Thwaite was moving about below, extinguishing all the lanterns except one. He placed it on the floor next to the chair with river carvings and sat down. He was holding a sketch pad. Wyn watched him open the pad and leaf slowly through the pages. One of his hands dropped down to the sides of the carved chair, his fingers tracing a pattern on the swirling lines. Gradually, the lantern's flame weakened to nothingness. The earth spirit closed his pad and shifted the chair to face the door.

Pulling a blanket around her, Wyn settled next to the window with its swaying cobweb pane that looked out onto the reservoir. The moon was little more than a sliver now and Wyn could sense it waning, moment by moment drawing summer to a close. Every so often, a spider clambered over the silken pane; checking, renewing, checking. She was just starting to doze off, when she heard footsteps below her and the swish of branches.

Sitting up and peering out through the window, she saw Thwaite striding through the deep, fresh snow and onto the reservoir, a pickaxe over his shoulder. Pip bounded at his side. A long way out over the ice, Thwaite stopped and bent down on one knee, touching the frozen surface with his hand. Wyn saw the earth spirit's lips moving, as if he were talking to someone. He stood up, turning slowly and staring long and hard around him. Then Wyn saw his axe blade glint in the moonlight as it flashed down onto the ice. Shards exploded around him. With metronomic timing, the earth spirit struck the ice again and again.

Wind blew around Wyn and then Tawhir was sitting beside her, looking out through the window. His face, shielded by his long hair, was so close to her that if he turned towards her, their noses would touch. His breath stirred the cobweb window panes.

Wyn resisted the temptation to glance towards the boy.

"Go away," she muttered, but Tawhir didn't budge. He kept watching the earth spirit's efforts out on the reservoir.

"I told him not to exert himself trying to heal your friend. And he's got no better chance of releasing his girlfriend from the ice."

"What are you on about?"

"A water spirit; I've hardly seen one more beautiful. I don't know how he did it. She must have a thing for bad-tempered earthers."

"What happened to her?"

"When the reservoir froze, she was trapped under the surface; a terrible thing for a water spirit. They are born to movement; ceaseless travelers of earth and sky."

The platform shifted as Tawhir got to his feet, stepping away from her. She glanced around but to her annoyance the boy had his back to her.

"Don't wait up, Mugasa."

"Where are you going?"

"To look for your enemies."

"I thought you said that was dangerous."

"I changed my mind."

"Will you just wait?"

At her outburst of temper, the boy turned around, one hand pushing his long hair from his face. Wyn's chest tightened. There was something so familiar about the way he'd just done that. He was a stranger and yet she recognized his every movement, his every expression. And why did she feel so completely drawn to him, and so angry with him at the same time? What the hell had gone on between them?

Tawhir turned from her again.

"Get some sleep. You'll need it for your training."

"When will you be...?"

But the wind spirit was already gone. Overhead, hawthorn leaves shook and the family of owls complained. Wyn squinted through the cobweb window, trying to catch a glimpse of where he was going. All she saw was a faint movement in the sky and clouds parting, then closing behind him.

Outside, the sound of Thwaite's pickaxe striking the frozen lake rang through the night.

15

"Ten years. That was how long I was trained by the earth spirit who was here before me," Thwaite told Wyn as they stepped out of the hawthorn house into stillness and the grays of dawn.

He strode away at breakneck speed towards Pateley Bridge and Wyn had to run to keep pace with him, her eyes continually on the sky. Overnight, her eyesight had miraculously sharpened. She could easily see Tawhir now, impossibly high up, billowing between clouds.

"Ten years to learn the knowledge that she'd accumulated since before these hills were ever formed. Do you know what she told me on her last day, as she lay down to rest in the heather? We've barely scratched the surface, she said. And now here I am, with two days to teach you everything I know about the earth and all the other elements. I'd best take some shortcuts. And we'd best both hope that you have some talent."

Like the night before, Thwaite led her into tunnels and through thickets, but this time they also climbed up branches that were as close together as steps and walked along a path in the canopy of trees by the river, much to the entertainment of the jackdaws and crows chattering at them from their frosty nests.

As much as Wyn had a sense of wonder to be passing through the dale on Thwaite's secret paths, she couldn't escape the feeling that she was somehow betraying herself. With every footstep, unease grew in her. She felt trapped, not wanting to go on, but not knowing why.

From the treetops, Wyn could see clear across the dale. Her gaze flicked up to Highdale, then panned around the other houses and on towards the high school. All her life she'd felt uncomfortable in this world of people, feeling alien and alone and never knowing why. In less than a day she had crossed into the world of the spirits. Now, with every footstep, she felt like she was casting off her old life and the few bonds that tied her to it; even Robin, even Kate.

But even as she thought this, she saw Kate swinging Thwaite's axe at the ice spirit and remembered all the times Robin had helped her and Mrs. March. Angry with herself, Wyn moved on through the treetops behind the earth spirit, doing her best to remember all the love she had known from Mrs. March, Robin and Kate.

The trees vibrated as her fingers brushed against them. When the jackdaws chattered, Wyn found that she half understood them.

They reached Skrikes Wood just as the sun appeared over the hilltops. Climbing down through the roots of the ash, Thwaite led Wyn through a part of the cavern that she hadn't seen before: through meadows full of different orchids, their petals in the shape of bees, butterflies; through dog-rose bushes that were twined with blackberry thorns; a pond where a family of badgers were vigorously at work, widening the banks.

The earth spirit walked ahead of Wyn with his hands outstretched, brushing the plants and trees he passed. And all the time, bees and butterflies bobbed by his cheeks and birds landed on his bare forearms, jostling for attention. He came to an abrupt stop by unkempt bushes of dog roses, their thorny stems tumbling onto purple bugle that grew in their shadow.

"Touch is the language of plants, of trees, of all living things," he said, carefully taking a bee in his hand, his thumb brushing the tips of its wings. "It is how most ordinary earth spirits communicate with nature." Thwaite's eyes gleamed momentarily and the bee rose into the air, circling around Wyn. Now Thwaite reached out to a dog-rose bush, his eyes gleaming again, and Wyn watched with a shiver of delight as the bush drew back the thorny stems that were choking the flowers beneath them.

"I am an ordinary earth spirit. The range of my power is limited to what I can touch," continued Thwaite. "Only the very greatest among my kind can communicate with nature by thought alone, reading the mind of any creature or plant in their territories. I know of only five living earth spirits with this power: Sagarmatha and Denali, the mountain lords;

Uluru in the east; and the forest lords Amazonia and Kongo. Yet you, Wyn, you have a strength infinitely greater than any of them. You have the power to send your thoughts across oceans, across continents, to shake mountains on the other side of the world. It is this power that you need to rediscover before tomorrow night, before the last chance of summer is gone."

"No pressure then," muttered Wyn.

"In the first year of my training, I learned how to communicate with nature; to speak with the plants and animals of the territory that one day I would inherit. Let's see how you get on."

"How long do I have?"

"Until lunchtime. Now, hold out your hands."

Then, with a momentary gleam of his green eyes, all the birds, bees and butterflies that had been clustering around him flew to Wyn, landing on her arms, hands, shoulders, and she even found herself looking into the waggling antennae of a butterfly that had come to rest on her nose.

The next few hours were the most surreal and exhilarating of Wyn's life.

Thwaite threw challenge after challenge at her. Every time she was sure she was going to fail. After all, how on earth was she expected to suddenly be able to have a conversation with a family of moles? Or be able to walk into the center of the bee glade and peer into their hives and not be stung by any of the hundreds of thousands of creatures that buzzed around her? And yet, under Thwaite's instruction, she was able to understand all the animals in the cavern and they could understand her. It happened slowly at first and then with an ease that was as bewildering to Wyn as it was wondrous.

Now that she could communicate with all the creatures of the cavern, Wyn found herself wondering if she hadn't always understood them a little. How many times had she sat on the windowsill of her bedroom at Mrs. March's house, letting the birdsong from Spring Wood come in with the breeze? While she hadn't known what the birds were saying, Wyn had always been able to recognize their individual voices and had always been able to sense their mood, and the mood of the wood itself. The birds had been her friends, even as she'd kept her distance from other children at school.

If the earth spirit was as astonished at the speed of Wyn's progress as she was, he said nothing. All that Wyn noticed was a new vigor in his long stride and the occasional narrowing of his eyes.

Leaving the hives, he had told her to take off her boots, and now Wyn walked barefoot through the grass and flowers. Under her feet, the ground had suddenly become a living thing, vibrating with an energy just like the one she'd felt within the trees. With every step she took, her feet seemed to press deeper into the ground and the power of the earth rose up in her, making her limbs feel lighter and stronger. She had barely slept last night and walked far already today, but now all the tiredness washed away from Wyn and she felt like she could walk forever.

And all around her were the voices of animals, which now she could understand.

After the animals, Thwaite led her from flower to flower, watching as she carefully stroked their stems. They were harder to understand than the trees. The images they showed her were dreamlike and fleeting; a blur of rain, wind, the darkness of the soil. Hardest of all was a harebell, the last flower that Thwaite led her to. Long minutes passed until it responded to Wyn's touch and she was able to see into the flower's mind.

When she looked up, Thwaite was leaning on his axe.

"Did it show you things?" he asked.

Wyn nodded.

"All my life, I've not got anything out of them. What did it have to say?"

"Much the same as the others," replied Wyn, which made the earth spirit chuckle.

"Obstinate little flowers," he muttered.

And not for the first time that day, Wyn noticed the glimmer of excitement in the earth spirit's eyes and a familiar warning ached in her heart. But Wyn was too caught up in the pleasure of talking to the animals and plants to listen to the voice warning her to leave the cavern and forget what the earth spirit had taught her.

After lunch, Thwaite slung a heavy bag over his shoulder and, carrying Pip under his arm, led Wyn up the ladder of vines. They clambered out into stillness and a silver disc of a sun, shrouded in cloud.

"Now that you can talk to plants and trees, let's see if you can be of use to them," said the earth spirit. He led

Wyn into a dell of beech trees, dark and heavy with decay, and told her to lay her hands on the trees. They stirred at Wyn's touch, vibrating faintly and showing blurry, broken images. Wyn remembered Mrs. March in hospital, right at the end. The old woman had curled her fingers around Wyn's hand. Her voice had been little more than breaths.

"We've got to help them," she told Thwaite.

Nodding, the earth spirit took an earthenware pot out of his bag. It was full of the same purple paste he had rubbed onto Kate after the bear's attack. The smell of wildflowers and warm summer days rose up from the pot.

"What's in it?" Wyn asked.

"Betony, knapweed, hawthorn berries, among others. On its own it has some strength, but in the right hands ... take some."

He watched as Wyn scooped out some of the paste, frowning at first, then breathing out deeply when the paste began to glimmer between Wyn's fingers. The glimmer became a sparkle, washing over her hands, casting the dell in purple light. Thwaite dipped his fingers into the pot and held them up to show her, raising his eyebrows. At his touch, the paste shone, but with nothing like the intensity that it did against Wyn's skin.

Under the earth spirit's guidance, Wyn went from tree to tree in the dell, dabbing the paste on their frosted trunks until she felt their vibrations become stronger and steadier. With every tree she touched, Wyn felt her strength grow. Frost melted from their trunks, snow fell from their branches.

As she reached into the earthenware pot for more paste, Thwaite drew it away from her.

"Try it without this time," he said.

It was harder without the paste, much harder. The trees were slower to respond to her. Sweat pricked her eyes and tiredness dragged at her limbs, but Wyn kept thinking of Mrs. March and Kate, and the memory of them drove her on. Pip stayed by her side, encouraging her, and more than once Wyn steadied herself by resting her hand on the collie's head. She was breathing deeply when she clambered out of the dell behind Thwaite.

The earth spirit was leaning against his axe, looking at the silver birches higher up the wood.

"Now them," he said, nodding up at the slender trees.

To Wyn's irritation, he hadn't thanked her or shown any acknowledgment of what she had already done. Glaring at him, she set off towards the trees, only to be held back by one of the earth spirit's huge hands.

"No, heal them from here," he said.

"But I can't touch them from here."

"You don't need to. Reach out to them with your will alone."

Wyn was so tired after her efforts in the dell that she wanted nothing more than to slump down on the snow. As she planted her feet and looked up towards a single silver birch, she heard a warning voice from within. Ignoring it, Wyn reached with her senses towards the distant tree.

Nothing. She felt nothing.

The voice grew stronger, angrier.

Summoning all the energy in her body, Wyn stretched out her hands, imagining her fingers stretching over the snow and clasping the slim trunk. Did she feel something this time? Did the faintest of tremors come from the tree? It was gone as soon as it came, leaving her gasping for breath.

Now the voice was raging through her, telling her over and over to stop.

"Keep going," said Thwaite.

"I'm trying."

"Try harder."

"What the hell do you know?!"

Wyn focused with all her might on the tree. But as she did, the voice in her mind reached a new level of fury and suddenly the wood dissolved around her and she was hurtling up, up into a blood-red sky. Anger and fear coursed through her body, driving her on, away from her glittering assailant. Glancing back, she saw glimpses of tapering diamond wings, great silver eyes, white fire. The sky was growing darker. A shimmering wall of light appeared. She hurtled towards it, oblivious to him, to her own fear. There was pain, dazzling light. And blackness.

Then she was back in the wood, on her knees in the snow, gasping for air. Thwaite looked anxiously down at her.

"Forgive me. I was pushing you too hard."

"What if I can't be Mugasa again?"

"In a single morning, you've mastered what took me five years. You can become her once more, I'm sure of that."

"What if I don't want to be her?"

"What just happened? What did you see?"

"Tell me about Sh'en Shiekar," gasped Wyn.

16

A barren hilltop. In the distance, the frozen sea. Denali stood with his back to it, watching dark specks moving on faraway fields. He glanced upwards. A moment later Foehn fell from the sky, landing noiselessly in front him.

"Sh'en Shiekar is gone. The winds don't speak of him," she said.

The huge earth spirit took her in his arms.

"He may have found her," he said.

"Then we've lost!"

"Even if he has tracked Mugasa down, bringing her back to power will be no simple task, especially if she remembers her past."

"Do you think she would?"

"To be reborn is to be reshaped, not cast anew. However deep her memories of a past life may lie, they will be inside her," said Denali. "Do not forget that she has remained hidden for so long. A part of her does not want to return.

The same part that made her give up her powers in her last life. We've not lost. The odds are still with us. What news of the others?"

"Sirmik and Oya have found nothing."

"Are there no living earth spirits to the west?"

"Only a few still walk the land, but they work alone."

"And Kaniq?"

"He, too, has vanished."

"So this is why my wolves are returning," said the earth spirit. The distant specks had become shapes, bounding across white fields. One of the wolves ran ahead of the others. As he looked towards the pack leader, Denali's eyes gleamed. After a few moments of silence, he breathed out deeply.

"There is a valley to the south, where Kaniq's tracks end. An earth spirit lives there. He has a girl with him."

"A human child? It can't be her. Of all forms, she'd never have chosen to come back as a human."

"It wouldn't have been her doing the choosing. No, if it is Mugasa, the earth has brought her back in the form she most disliked," said Denali.

"To punish her?"

"Or to help her. There is sense to this, but it would be a dangerous path."

"I will go to the valley and see her for myself."

"No, Foehn. If Sh'en Shiekar has tracked her down, he'll be watching for any threat to her."

"Then what? We can't leave her alone, hoping that the earth spirit, or even Sh'en Shiekar himself, will be unable to return her to power."

"We have no control over Sh'en Shiekar, but the earth spirit can be stopped, though not by you."

The wolf pack had almost reached the two spirits. Their leader padded forward. Denali crouched down, caressing the wolf's ears.

When he finished talking, the wolf sprang away, calling to the others. Denali watched the pack return the way they had come. Foehn slipped her hand in his.

Dipping a finger in the purple paste, Thwaite drew a symbol in the snow. Wyn felt a shiver run through her when she saw what he had made.

"You recognize the symbol, don't you?" said Thwaite.

"What is it?" whispered Wyn.

"Yin and yang, the mark of the two dragons. The dark swirl represents the fire dragon, and the white is the ice dragon. The two are soulmates, born in each other's arms. The dots represent their hearts. The white dot is Sh'en Shiekar's heart, which he has given to you. The dark dot is your heart, which he now holds. He is your equal, your eternal other."

As he spoke, Wyn heard a faint roar of wind, calling over and over. *Mugasa.* Now that she recognized the voice, Wyn realized that she had heard it all her life, whispering in and out of her dreams, searching for her. It was the voice that she'd always pushed away, often waking with a start in her bed at Mrs. March's house, then at Highdale, alone in the stillness of the night.

She bent down to the yin-yang symbol, tracing over it with a finger.

"His heart in mine. And mine in his," she whispered.

"He'll be out there, somewhere in the world," said Thwaite. "Can you sense him?"

As much as she felt a great longing to search for the owner of the voice, a part of Wyn resisted looking for him. She was torn between the two emotions, before, finally, she shut her eyes and whispered his name, "Sh'en Shiekar."

Everything was speed and light and sky. Her thoughts rushed over snowbound towns, glinting in the afternoon sun, through clouds hurried along by stiff winds. Wyn saw a huge man with dark hair that fell to his shoulders, and a stern-faced woman at his side. They were striding through a frozen wood. Then she was rising up high above the storm clouds and she saw Tawhir staring downwards at the man and the woman. As she watched him, Wyn saw Tawhir look up, searching this way and that. Was something coming through the clouds? Was he looking towards her?

Wyn tore her thoughts away, opening her eyes and replying to Thwaite, "No, I can't."

"You're sure?"

It was just the boy her thoughts turned to, not a dragon, and she hated herself for it.

"I said I was."

The earth spirit was shaking his head.

"No, I don't believe it. The love between the dragons is legendary. For thousands of years the world has changed, but at the center of things was always you and he; always together, as you were from the first. Though you have been reborn, you are still Mugasa. You must still be able to sense him."

"I CAN'T! I WON'T!" Wyn yelled, and for a split second there was a change in her voice. A wildness, the roar of wind. Gold light glowed in the trees around her. They trembled. The earth spirit was rocked back. He fastened one great hand on the closest tree trunk, the other reaching for Pip, who pressed herself to his legs.

The anger left Wyn's body, leaving her suddenly exhausted. She reached out to Pip, but the collie stayed close to Thwaite, watching her from the corner of an eye.

"There is another story told of your death," said the earth spirit, stroking Pip's head. "One that tells of a terrible rift between you and Sh'en Shiekar. It is said that you fought over what was happening to the world. While he refused to take action against humans, you hated the destruction they were causing and had secretly begun backing the rebel spirits. Not long afterwards you died."

"Was it him? Did he kill me?"

"This story is only a rumor. No one knows if it's true."

"But you believe it, don't you?"

"No, I don't," said Thwaite, but Wyn saw the tension in his face.

Just then, Pip gave a low growl and the earth spirit glanced up. He held a finger to his lips and stepped close to Wyn, his eyes gleaming momentarily.

John and his father were coming slowly towards them, staring up into the branches of every tree they passed.

"There's no buds coming that I can see," said David Ramsgill. "And what about these bees? Where are they?"

"They were here. You saw the photos," insisted John. His father frowned at him.

"That I did."

"They were coming out from under an ash."

"The tree was probably rotten and the bees made their hive in its trunk."

"The tree was fine. It's around here somewhere. I just can't ..." As John scanned the wood, he looked straight at Wyn. She was sure he would see her, and for a brief moment his gaze paused, before moving on.

"I can't stop the quarrying for the sake of some bees. Even if they've survived up until now, they won't for much longer."

"You just don't care, do you?"

"I've got fifteen men relying on me for work. Most of them have got families. I've got to think of them."

"There's more to life than money."

"John, don't be so naive."

"I'm not."

"Yes, you are. There's precious little work around here. What do you think will happen if my business goes under? We might be all right for a while, but many of my men won't be able to stay in the dale. They'll have to head for the cities and fight for whatever scraps are there. And I wouldn't wish that on anyone."

"There must be some other way."

David Ramsgill suddenly tilted his head in Wyn and Thwaite's direction, frowning, his eyes flicking between them and the purple stain on the snow.

"I wish there was, but there's not," he said, starting to walk towards them. "If it's not me quarrying Skrikes Wood, it'll be someone else. Better it's done locally, to benefit local people."

He stopped just a few paces away, so close that the puffs of condensation from his breath blew around Wyn. Just then, one of the earth spirit's blackbirds swooped out of the trees, passing so close to his face that David Ramsgill stepped back in surprise. The bird landed on the branch of an oak, close to John, and began chattering.

With a last, hard look in Wyn's direction David Ramsgill turned back to his son.

"We'd best be getting home."

"I want to keep looking."

"There's nothing to see. Come on, John."

David Ramsgill began making his way downhill through the wood. Wyn saw the boy's shoulders fall. He put his hands in his pockets and followed his father. The iron gate clanged. Wyn watched father and son walking along the road to Bewerley.

"How did they not see us?" said Wyn.

"I had them thinking that we were a tree stump. It wasn't easy, mind. That one's got the gift."

"John?"

"In time, perhaps. It often passes from parent to child. For now it's his father who has the gift, though he doesn't use it."

"David Ramsgill?" said Wyn, astonished. "But if that's true, you could tell him about the wood, you could make him stop the quarrying."

"He's closed his heart to the earth. Only when his

heart opens will his eyes follow suit."

"What if his heart doesn't open? You'll stand by and watch Skrikes Wood be destroyed?"

"There are rules that govern my kind; rules that I can't break, however much I might want to. All I can do is try to open the hearts of humans through the beauty of the territories we protect."

"Even now?" said Wyn, taking in the snowbound landscape, the deep smell of decay in the wood.

"I'll keep my faith in the earth and in the opening of hearts," said Thwaite. "Summer isn't over yet."

All of a sudden Wyn's stomach lurched and Tawhir landed with a thump beside her. The wind fell silent. What snow was still in the air drifted down, clinging to the wind spirit's dark clothes.

"What did that boy want?" demanded Tawhir.

Was he jealous? The idea that he was pleased Wyn.

"None of your business," she replied, suppressing a smile at his evident annoyance. "So where have you been?"

"We have unwelcome visitors, not far from here. An ice spirit and a fire spirit to the west and an earth spirit to the east; one who can move the land with his mind alone."

Thwaite's face tightened.

"Describe him."

"Brown skin, long hair to his shoulders, stronger than any earther I've ever seen."

"Denali," muttered Thwaite. "The greatest earth spirit of the Americas."

"That was my guess," said Tawhir.

Wyn recalled the enormous man she'd seen in her mind's eye, in the frozen wood.

"Do you think he's joined the rebel spirits?" said Thwaite.

"Has he joined them or is he leading them? We'll know soon enough. He's heading in this direction."

"Towards Nidderdale?"

"Wyn can stop him."

"She's not ready."

"What have you been doing with her all day? Hugging trees? Letting her hang out with her boyfriend? Wake up, earther! Summer ends tomorrow night and Denali may be here sooner than that. We need Mugasa back. If you can't help Wyn, I will. It's time she learned about wind."

Tawhir's gray eyes fixed on Wyn, making her feel as uncomfortable as she'd ever felt around him.

"In your past life you were the greatest of all flyers. It is said that you could cross the world in under an hour and silence hurricanes with a single thought. What do you say, Wyn. Will you let me show you what you've forgotten?"

Tawhir held out his hand to her, and though all of Wyn's instincts rose up in her, warning her to refuse him, she imagined the boy racing into the sky above the dale and had a fierce longing to be flying with him.

"All right. I'll do it," she said.

17

❖❖❖❖

"There are three groups of winds you must learn to control," said Tawhir, his long hair streaming behind him. They had climbed to the top of Skrikes Wood and onto an outcrop that was known in the dale as Eagle Rock. Minute by minute, the winds had picked up, lifting snow from the treetops and casting it over the dale

"The weakest are the low, local winds," continued Tawhir, "hardly more than gusts and breezes that skim fields and brush through woods. Above them are the middle winds, capricious and changeable, dominating most of the sky. The last group are the high winds, known as the dragon winds; great torrents of air that flow across the uppermost reaches of the atmosphere. They are strongest of all winds and the hardest to control. A handful of wind spirits have some sway over them, but only the dragons can truly dominate them."

Beside Tawhir, Thwaite stood with his axe at the ready, glancing in all directions.

"I hope you know what you're doing, boy. Bringing Wyn out here, in the open, when Denali and who knows who else are coming …"

"Is a risk we have to take. Summer ends tomorrow and I can't teach her about wind in your hole under the wood. So you keep watching and let me do the teaching."

There was an authority to Tawhir now that Wyn had only seen glimpses of before. All of his irreverence and flippancy had gone. Somehow she knew that this was the true Tawhir that she was seeing, and it made him more familiar to her than ever.

"Wyn, are you listening?"

"Three kinds of winds. Got it!"

"Then show me. Call out to the winds all around us and silence them."

Wyn glanced around at the enormity of her task; at the trees bent under the whip of the gale. She was being buffeted where she stood, snow stinging her bare legs and face. Her heart was pounding wildly, both in warning and in excitement. How many times in her childhood had she rushed outside in storms and whirled around, imagining herself bending the storm to her will. Had she had this power all along? She flung up her hands to the sky, calling out in a clear, strong voice to the winds, telling them to become calm.

They blew on, oblivious to her.

"What do you think you're doing?" interjected Tawhir.

"What you told me."

"I told you to silence the winds! This isn't earth you're dealing with, or water. Winds only understand strength. Dominate them, force them to obey your will."

Wyn was filled with an overwhelming desire to force the boy off the rock. If he saw her anger, he ignored it, instead moving directly behind her and stretching an arm next to her cheek, so she could see where he was pointing.

"You see them? Four low winds and, higher up, two middle winds," he said, his voice loud in her ear as he jabbed his finger at different parts of the sky.

Doing her best not to be distracted by his closeness, Wyn concentrated on the storm. At first it was chaos to her. It sounded like all the birds of the cavern calling and chattering together, their voices a cacophony of dawn chorus. But slowly, with the utmost effort, the different shrieks and howls of the winds became clear to Wyn. There were half a dozen winds jumbled up in the sky — two middle winds, competing with each other to see who could blow hardest, and four low winds, racing excitedly about like spring hares, jostling each other up and down the sides of the dale and boxing at the walls and the woods.

"Yes," said Tawhir in her ear, "you have them now. Take the middle winds first."

Not wanting to be told what to do, Wyn reached her thought out to the low winds, commanding them to grow quiet. She felt them check a little, becoming aware of her, before scampering away with howls of defiance. Wyn grew angry. As she did, she felt her will strengthen. Now the low winds did take note of her, forced to abandon their wild play. They came unwillingly, fighting to be rid of her command, and it took all of Wyn's stubbornness and anger to make them obey her. Reluctantly they became still, obeying her will even as they were fighting it.

Now Wyn reached upwards, where the two stronger winds raced through the sky, wilder than ever, herding clouds that cast shadows over the dale. And Wyn now knew why Tawhir had told her to take them first; the middle winds were aware of her presence and were going to do their utmost to evade her.

"You're losing them," said Tawhir.

Even though he had stopped pointing, he was still pressed close to her, his breath on her cheek. Did some emotion pass between them? Or was it the wind that made him seem to rock a little on his feet?

He stepped away from her.

"The winds, Mugasa."

There was a coldness to his voice that rekindled Wyn's anger. She threw her will at the middle winds, but as she did, she lost her grip on the low winds and they sprang back to boisterous life. She brought them back under control and tried again with their more powerful siblings, but for all her efforts, every time she began to get a grip on the middle winds, the low winds escaped. Soon she was gasping for breath at the effort.

"What are you playing at, Mugasa?" shouted Tawhir at her side. "You used to rule the winds!"

"I'm trying!"

"Try harder!"

Wyn snapped her furious stare away from the boy and returned it to the sky. The two middle winds had raced way up, hiding in the clouds. With every last drop of her strong nature, Wyn went after them. She ordered the first wind to be silent. And at once the storm in the dale lessened dramatically. From the corner of her eye, she saw Thwaite and Tawhir's tense, upturned faces.

Now there was just the final middle wind left and it had no intention of being caught; bucking and twisting so her mind couldn't get a grip on it. The further from her the wind raced, the harder it was for Wyn to pursue it. And all the time the other winds she had calmed struggled to be free of her. Finally, with the last drop of her strength, Wyn seized the middle wind and brought it under control.

The dale was momentarily quiet. The snow that had been whipped up from the trees drifted down.

Then all six winds were fighting her at once and in their onslaught a lesser wind slipped from her grip, racing away over the river, leaving the alders rocking in its wake. Sensing weakness, all the other winds redoubled their efforts to break free.

"Hold them, Mugasa," said Tawhir.

She was trying, but already she felt her strength failing. Both middle winds were battering against her will. The strain was making her dizzy. She was losing them.

"Hold them!" yelled Tawhir.

Even as he was shouting at her, it was already too late. The five winds burst free from Wyn's will. The brief calm that had filled Nidderdale was lost in the renewed fury of their voices.

Her head spinning, Wyn dropped to her knees.

"Call them back," said Tawhir, catching Wyn's arm. She shook herself free, but he held her again in an iron grip.

"I can't," she gasped.

"Let go of her," said Thwaite, towering over Tawhir, but as he reached for the boy, one of the middle winds came hurtling down from the sky, skimming over the rock. The earth spirit was lifted off his feet and thrown into a snow-drift on the edge of Skrikes Wood. Wyn tried to go after him, but Tawhir held her back.

"What the hell are you doing?" she shouted, struggling to get free.

"What am I doing? What are you doing, Mugasa? Summer is almost over! There's no more time for your games!"

Tawhir lifted Wyn to her feet and wrapped his arms around her. His face was inches from her own.

"Let go of me!"

"Not until you've seen the world that you've created."

And suddenly the rock was shrinking beneath them.

Up and up they flew. The speed, the rush of air on her face, made Wyn's heart leap inside her.

This was a million times better than ice skating. She wanted to scream from the sheer joy of it. They were in clouds now, out of sight and in their own world.

"Want to go faster?" said Tawhir, his voice cutting through the roar of the storm.

"Yes!" said Wyn automatically, before quickly saying, "No!"

They rocketed upwards.

"I said no!" yelled Wyn, but Tawhir ignored her.

The clouds fell away. Golden sunlight burst around her. The dale was gone. They were in a luminous other world, cast in every shade of blue, so beautiful it made Wyn shiver. Tawhir stopped climbing. They hung there, weightless, in each other's arms.

Wyn looked up. Tawhir's face, only inches from hers, was perfectly still, his features like carved ice. His gleaming eyes looked into hers.

"This is where you belong, where you were born to be," said the boy.

"Take me down."

"You love it up here. It's all over your face."

And he was right. A part of Wyn wanted nothing more than to be up here above the world, with him. But still she felt an insistent warning.

"Please, take me down."

"Not yet, Mugasa," said Tawhir.

If he'd flown fast before, it was like a breeze next to the violence of this next climb. They sped upwards with a ferocity that took the breath from Wyn's lungs. Before she'd been holding Tawhir lightly at the waist. Now she had to put her arms around his neck, gripping with all her might. Tawhir was utterly concentrated on his task, seemingly oblivious to her. His face was still a mask. He barely seemed to be breathing. But she could feel his heart, pounding against hers.

Up, up, always up, as the sky turned from blue to purple and now to black. Tawhir's climb slowed to a glide. Wyn became aware of a shimmering wall of light coming towards them, identical to the wall she'd seen in the memory of her past life, and she was terrified. All her senses were screaming out for the boy not to cross the border.

To her relief, Tawhir did stop; just a hand's width away. He reached up, running his fingertips across it. Silver sparks fizzed down onto his sleeve. He watched them intently. His expression was impossible to read.

"The limit of our world," he said, his voice echoing in the deep silence around them.

"Touch it," he told her, turning his gleaming eyes towards her.

Wyn was afraid, but determined not to let Tawhir see her fear. She lifted her hand to touch the wall. There was a golden flash, and a jolt of electricity passed through her. She recoiled, startled, but only a moment later she stretched out her hand again, brushing it as lightly as she could across the wall. Specks of gold trailed from her fingers. She traced her hand close to Tawhir's.

"I catch the sun," she murmured. "You catch the moonlight."

Beyond their fingers, stars pulsed in the vastness of space.

Wyn had always been able to see the colors of the stars with her naked eye, as she looked from her bedroom window at Highdale. After the snows had begun to stay longer each year, leaching the color out of the dale, whenever Wyn had stared at the stars on clear nights, the multi-colored fairy lights of the heavens had made her heart sing. Now, from this new vantage point, they took her breath away. Wyn saw rings, clouds, flares of light, swirling gases. A star she had always thought pink turned out to be layer after layer of reds, whites, grays and golds.

"Look down, Mugasa," said Tawhir.

She did. Her breath froze on her lips.

Wyn inhaled sharply. No picture she'd seen had prepared her for this. It was the earth, but not an earth she recognized. Nearly everything was white. The two giant storms were spreading from each pole, covering most of the world

with their fury. Only Europe was still spared the full force
of the storm, but it was closing in quickly at the edges, raging
across boundary seas. Wyn had seen the frozen world on
TV, but from up here it was hideously real. Wyn saw a drop
of water fall past her feet, traveling silently downwards into
the dark. More drops fell. She realized she was crying.

She shut her eyes, whispering, "Take me home. Please."

"The whole earth is your home. And she needs you back,
Mugasa," said Tawhir, gripping her with a force that made
her glance up at him. As soon as she did, she knew it was
a mistake. Their eyes locked. She felt herself being drawn
towards him. When he spoke, he was so close to her that
his lips almost brushed against hers.

"We all need you back."

Wyn wanted to say she would go with the boy, let him
take her wherever he chose. But instead she squeezed her
eyes tight.

"I've tried. I can't."

She felt his breaths come even closer to her, then pull
sharply back.

"Fly well, Mugasa," Tawhir said, in a voice as hard as ice.
And he let go of her.

She was falling.

It was surreal at first. There was nothing around her but
the sky and rushing wind. She stretched out her arms and
legs, balancing herself so she fell flat and fast. The edges
of Europe vanished, then Italy, France, and she lost sight
of the frozen sea.

Clouds rose up and suddenly she slammed into them, her mouth filled with the taste of snow. She lost balance and began tumbling head over heels. She came out of the clouds backwards, fell briefly through clear air, then more clouds rushed and she was in them in a flash. Tumbling even quicker, she saw sky, the dale, clouds, dale, clouds ... she thought she was going to be sick. Tawhir appeared beside her.

"Are you trying to kill me?" she yelled, grabbing for him.

The boy kept just out of reach of Wyn's flailing hands.

"You were the world's greatest flyer, Mugasa."

"Help me!" yelled Wyn, catching a glimpse of Skrikes Wood. It was coming at her fast. This time, as she flailed for Tawhir, she felt wind come up beneath her arms. She stopped tumbling. She felt the wind underneath her. She was sure it was slowing her a little. Wyn concentrated on the wind, willing it to strengthen. Instead of obeying her, the wind weakened, slipping away. Angrily, Wyn called it back. At once it drove up into her, stopping her fall and suspending her, gasping with surprise. Tawhir drew alongside her.

"Now, command it," he told her.

But already the wind was straining away from her, trying to break free. In her confusion and panic, Wyn lost control of it.

Immediately, she was tumbling head over heels towards the dale. Tawhir caught up with her.

"Call it back!" he cried.

But everything was a blur to Wyn. The only thing she could focus on was the boy's gleaming eyes.

The wood was becoming enormous. She fell past the line of the moors. There was only a few hundred feet between her and the ground.

"MUGASA! FLY!"

She watched the treetops rush up to meet her. Wyn could feel winds all around her, like fires waiting to ignite. She flailed her arms, trying to grab them. The winds eluded her. She shut her eyes.

18

Not a soul was stirring in Pateley Bridge and only a few lights showed behind curtained windows as Wyn and Thwaite, with Pip trotting by his side, passed along the shadows of the riverbank and on through thickets and tunnels, until they were trudging along the bank of the reservoir.

Wyn moved as quickly and quietly as Thwaite now, though she paid little attention to how strong her body felt and how her bare feet made almost no impression on the snow beneath them. While the earth spirit glanced around constantly, pausing every now and then as one by one his blackbirds came looping through the heavy snowfall, landing on his outstretched hand, Wyn remained consumed by her thoughts.

At the last possible moment, Tawhir had caught her. Silently, he'd lowered her to the ground, and for the first time she'd seen true shock and sadness on his face. Letting her go, he'd vanished once more.

His words played over in her mind.

"The world that you've created," Tawhir had said. The world that she had created. When the storm eclipsed the world, there would be no turning back. After tomorrow night, there would be no more summers.

She couldn't turn back the snow. It was too much. For a brief time that day she'd started to believe in something, started to take joy in her newfound powers. But it was just a few animals she'd spoken to, only a handful of trees that she'd helped. And all the while she had been fighting against a voice inside, telling her to stop.

Wyn's bare feet slipped in the snow. She clung to a tree. Far across the dale, a light showed in Highdale. It was Robin. He'd opened a bedroom window and was looking out into the night. Despite being over a mile away, Wyn could see the lines in his face, the whiteness of his hands on the sill. Joan appeared at his side, tears on her cheeks. Robin drew back, closing the window. A curtain extinguished the light.

Pip padded forward, pressing her body against Wyn's legs. She rubbed the collie's ears, hearing the dog's worried, questioning thoughts in her mind.

"One minute I had a normal life, minding my own business, and now the world is going to hell and it's all my fault. Why does this have to be all on me?"

"Because you're Mugasa," said Thwaite.

"I didn't ask to be her. What if I don't want to be her? What if I'm happy just being Wyn?"

The earth spirit stood very still, momentarily glancing towards the frozen reservoir.

"Is that what you want?"

"I want Kate to be better. I want summer to come back. I …" Once again the warning voice filled her mind and shook her body. She broke off, gasping for breath.

"What is your heart telling you?" said Thwaite.

"I don't know."

But she did, though she was reluctant to admit it.

"You don't want to be Mugasa again, do you? That's why you've hidden all these years, why even now you're holding back your true power."

Wyn was going to keep up her denial, but she saw that there was no anger or criticism in the earth spirit's lean face. The longer she knew him, the more like Robin he seemed to her.

"What happened to you, child? Was it Sh'en Shiekar?"

Wyn clung harder to the tree.

"Sometimes I see glimpses of things. A cave in the mountains, sunset, something tearing at me. I don't know. Nothing makes much sense. And all you and Tawhir are saying is that everything bad is all my fault, that unless I become this … this all-powerful dragon before tomorrow night, every living thing is going to die! And I'm trying, I am, but I just can't. Why does it have to be all on me?"

"There might be another way to lift the cold, one that the rebel spirits long for above all else," said the earth spirit. "Though it would come at a terrible cost."

"What is it?"

"If you can't return, Sh'en Shiekar could …"

Thwaite's words froze on his lips. He wheeled around, his hands tightening on his axe. Beside Wyn, Pip stiffened and let out a low growl.

Wolves.

They were streaming out of a wood on the hillside, leaping a stone wall and surging towards the reservoir. They pulled up ten feet from Wyn and Thwaite, under the alders and bramble bushes that lined the frozen water. Muscles twitched in their long gray bodies. Their jaws were slack, tasting the air.

"Stay back," said Thwaite, pushing Wyn behind him. She watched the earth spirit walk towards the wolves, his eyes gleaming green.

"How dare you come at me like this, in my territory?"

The pack leader, a rangy beast of a creature, gave a whine that showed his teeth and continued towards them, his mate at his side. The remaining wolves fanned out behind the lead pair. With no warning, the pack leader sprang towards Thwaite. Quick as a flash, Pip leapt to meet him.

"Pip! Come back!" yelled Thwaite as wolf and dog slammed into each other and rolled in the snow, frenziedly snapping and snarling.

Thwaite bent to the ground, closing his eyes. A moment later, bramble stems whipped out of the bushes past Wyn's feet and caught the wolf leader's back legs, dragging the animal off Pip. The brambles wrapped tightly around the wolf. The creature howled as the thorny stems bit into his flesh. Now the entire wolf pack threw themselves at Thwaite. He fought them off with his axe as more brambles shot out, tangling themselves around the wolves and pulling them to the ground. Just as Wyn thought Thwaite had the upper hand, she heard Pip barking and saw a second wolf pack, at least ten-strong, bounding through the snow. The earth spirit was turning to face them when Wyn saw the original wolf leader bite his way free from his bonds and leap at Thwaite as his back was turned. Wyn shouted and he spun round, swinging his axe. But the wolf was too quick. The animal leaped at Thwaite's chest, sinking his teeth into the earth spirit's shoulder.

As Thwaite was grappling with the wolf, the second pack visibly picked up their pace. Pip bounded forward. Just in time, Wyn flung herself onto the collie to hold her back. Rolling over, her arms still clamped around Pip, Wyn frantically looked for a way to stop the second pack. They were running up to a row of alders at the edge of the reservoir. With no chance of reaching the trees before the wolves, Wyn threw her will towards the trees, demanding they come to her aid. Nothing happened. The wolves were running underneath them now. In moments, they would reach the earth spirit.

"Please!" Wyn yelled. Energy coursed through her body, pouring forth from her outstretched hand. Suddenly she felt the trees' vibrations. Her mind joined with theirs.

Immediately the alders' dark branches bent down and wrapped around the wolves. Directing her will towards the thicket, Wyn sent brambles whipping around the wolf that was attacking Thwaite, binding the animal's limbs and dragging him off the earth spirit.

Releasing Pip, Wyn ran to help Thwaite. His face was waxy and his breath was coming in short rasps. He was glancing between Wyn and the wolves she'd entangled, snarling, in the alders. Thwaite started to say something, then the light left his eyes and he collapsed on the snow.

Blood was pouring from the earth spirit's shoulder. Panicking, Wyn pressed her hands against the wound, trying to stop the flow, but the blood kept seeping though her fingers. Hurrying, she fumbled through Thwaite's pack, prised off the lid of an earthenware jar. There was just enough purple paste in the bottom to coat Wyn's fingers. As she'd done with the trees, Wyn rubbed the paste between her hands until it sparkled and then rubbed the mixture into Thwaite's shoulder. The blood flow slowed and a little color returned to the earth spirit's face, but try as she might to revive him, he didn't wake.

Pip growled and paced around her and Thwaite. Some of the wolves were already biting their way through the branches that bound them. Wyn knew that there was nothing else to do. She would have to carry him.

Wyn put her shoulder under one of the earth spirit's arms and hauled him off the ground. It was like trying to pick up a tree trunk. Thwaite was a foot taller than her and knotted with muscles.

Wyn's legs buckled and she and the earth spirit were back on the snow. So close to her that she could feel the heat of his breaths, the wolf pack leader had almost gnawed his way free. Only a branch knotted around his hind leg was holding him back.

"TAWHIR!" she called up at the sky, searching the night as she did. Even though she couldn't see him, Wyn sensed that he was somewhere out there. She called his name again. Nothing. Wyn's temper flared.

And maybe because of her anger, or maybe because she had no time to think, but now Wyn was able to haul

Thwaite off the ground and over her shoulder. Only when she'd got him there did Wyn realize what she'd just done, and was still doing. Wyn took a step forward. Despite Thwaite's legs dragging through the snow, she found that she had the strength to carry him.

By the time they crashed through the entrance of Thwaite's home, the wolves were already streaming away from the reservoir, up into the moors. The pack leader hung back momentarily, hidden in the deep fastness of trees at the top of the dale, his bright eyes fixed on the tangle of brambles and hawthorn trees which Wyn had just disappeared into. Then he raced off after the others, heading east, back towards the way they had come.

19

In the dark hawthorn house, Wyn was being mobbed by animals.

All the occupants of the dresser and the sleeping platform had emerged and were clustering around the chair in which Wyn had laid Thwaite. The other animals made way to let the snakes onto the earth spirit. Wyn watched as one of them wrapped itself tightly around Thwaite's shoulder. But even though the wound bled less, there was still blood running over the snake's scales. Wyn knew that the animals alone couldn't heal Thwaite; they needed her help.

Hurriedly, Wyn started untying the burlap sacks which hung on the side wall. There were at least fifty, each full of dried wildflowers; some she recognized and others that were new to her. She went up and down the row of sacks, touching and smelling the flowers, trying to figure out which were the right ones for Thwaite's wound.

Wyn noticed the earth spirit's sketch pad on a shelf of the dresser and grabbed it, opening it in the hope that she might find some guide to the different wildflowers. There were no notes, only pictures. One page showed a beautifully drawn image of the meadow between Gouthwaite and Wath, overflowing with pink and white yarrow. The next depicted a grassy verge, intricately planted with species after species of wildflowers. Every page of the sketch pad revealed more of Thwaite's dreams for his territory. And amongst the images were sketches of a blue-eyed woman walking through the Nidd, through rainfall.

A fierce anger rose up in Wyn. She wasn't going to let him die. Slamming the book shut, she stood in front of the sacks and emptied her mind of everything but the wildflowers.

She pictured them in life, growing in the dale in some long-ago summer; their flowers unfurling under the sky and their thin roots grasping the earth. Wyn found that she was flying over them, so low that petals and stalks brushed against her. Everything was warmth, soft breezes, the scent of one flower to the next; yarrow and speedwell on a sunny bank, pimpernels in the shade of trees, clumps of foxgloves. When she reached out to them, she saw with a start that it was no longer with a human hand.

Suddenly Wyn was back in the hawthorn house, standing in front of the sacks. Even though she was sure she hadn't moved, she was holding a bunch of wildflowers. She scrunched them into a ball and rubbed them between her palms. Just a few seconds later, she opened her hands to find a sparkling green ointment in them.

She pressed her hands over Thwaite's wound until the paste stopped shimmering between her fingers. Thwaite's breathing became more regular. When she took away her hands, she saw that the gash was no longer bleeding and was starting to close up.

She looked for a blanket in the dresser. When she came back with it, rabbits and mice had pressed themselves into Thwaite's lap, the snakes were curled around his arms and the three blackbirds were perched on his good shoulder. Pip had settled herself at his feet, pressing her fur into his frost-mottled toes. Wyn laid the blanket over Thwaite's lower body, reminded of how she had once done this for Mrs March.

Wyn's heart quickened. Looking out of the cobweb window, she saw Tawhir streaking down from the stars. He crashed through the hawthorn canopy, landing beside Thwaite and examining the earth spirit's wound.

"What happened?" he asked. Wyn told him. The boy went to the dresser and lit a lamp. He examined Thwaite's wound, then turned to her.

"You did this all on your own? I'm impressed."

"Where the hell were you when we needed you?"

"There was a powerful wind spirit circling not far from here. She came after me, wanting to know what I was doing here. Who knows what side she was on, but I wasn't going to risk it. I was halfway across Europe before I managed to shake her off."

Wyn scowled at him. Only a few hours ago he'd dropped her from the edge of space. She still heard the wind howling, saw Tawhir pull away as she tried to grab onto him.

And now here he was, as if nothing had happened, sitting on the thyme floor with a lit lamp beside him, emptying his pockets. Instead of his usual junk food, there was a soft loaf, a round cheese wrapped in paper and a bag of white peaches that filled the room with their fragrance. They had always been Wyn's favorite fruit, although it had been years since she'd last had one. When he held out a peach to her, she reached for it, then, remembering her anger, quickly retracted her hand.

"Won't you join me?" said Tawhir.

"I'm fine where I am," replied Wyn. Was there a flash of genuine hurt on the boy's face? He bent forward to tear off a piece of bread and then a lump of the cheese, his eyes disappearing underneath a thick veil of hair.

"You know, you're just the same in this life as you were in the last."

Wyn's pulse began hammering wildly. She gripped hold of the back of Thwaite's chair, suddenly terrified to ask the question that had been burning in her mind these past days.

In as steady a voice as she could manage, she said, "How did we know each other?"

Did he react? Did the bread pause for a split second on the way to his mouth? Wyn was watching Tawhir's every tiny movement, but to her intense annoyance, the hair still remained across his face, hiding whatever expression he might be showing. It was an age before he finished his mouthful.

"We were friends," he replied. And again, there was the same lack of emotion in his voice. He tore off another hunk of bread and some cheese. "Don't you remember?"

Friends? Wyn couldn't imagine being friends with Tawhir. Kate was the only friend Wyn had ever had, unless she counted John, and that was awkward most of the time. When she didn't reply, Tawhir turned his head a fraction towards her.

"Perhaps you will remember one day," he said.

Thwaite stirred in his chair, his breathing becoming labored. As Wyn bent over the earth spirit, a soft wind blew around the hawthorn house, rocking the leaves of the trees. Tawhir was standing beside her.

"You've got to get it just right," he told her. "Too much and they'll get annoyed. Too little and they won't ..."

He paused, concentrating.

"Won't what?"

"Find their voices."

A faint noise began to rise around them. Amongst the sound of wind and rustling leaves, impossibly far off and as delicate as moths' wings, Wyn heard something quite distinct and magical. The sound sent shivers down her spine.

"Are they...?"

"Yes, trees can sing, when they are in a mood to. I've heard a whole forest break into song when a new earth spirit has been born within it. When you return to us, the joy of the trees will echo across the whole world."

Thwaite took a deep, contented breath and returned to sleep. Tawhir picked up the earth spirit's sketch pad and began slowly leafing through it.

"Have you never wondered why you were reborn here, in this unremarkable territory? Of all the territories in the world the earth could have chosen, why this one? And why him? A more powerful spirit might have found you years earlier, and would certainly be able to train you better. But no, she brought you back from death and placed you here, in human form, with no memory of who you once were. It's almost as if ..."

The boy looked up from the book, the light fading from his eyes. Wind died in the leaves and the hawthorns ceased their song. Thwaite's house fell into shadows and the stillness of night.

"As if what?"

"She was giving you a choice."

As Tawhir spoke the words, an old anger started to beat through Wyn.

"I was reborn here, with no memory. How the hell is that giving me a choice?" she demanded.

"She could have brought you back in your true form, with all your power intact. But instead she hid you from us, and from yourself. She has placed the fate of the world in your hands. What will your choice be, Mugasa? Will you return to us and end this long winter?"

He didn't look at her as he spoke, but kept slowly turning the pages of the sketch pad. She remembered what Thwaite had said just before the wolves attacked.

"Thwaite said that it wasn't all up to me."

Tawhir's hand froze on the pages of the pad.

"What did the earther tell you?"

"He said there was another way. Something to do with Sh'en Shiekar."

"He's wrong."

Wyn knew the boy was lying.

"Tell me."

"It doesn't matter. You will come back."

"Just tell me what it is!"

"If you don't return to power before summer ends tomorrow night, only Sh'en Shiekar can restore the balance of nature. He will follow the path that you took and give up his power."

"Would that kill him?"

"What choice does he have? It's not just his life, but the life of every human on the planet."

Thrusting the pad into her hands, Tawhir strode out of Thwaite's house, walking quickly across the frozen reservoir. She glanced down at the pad. It was open on a page showing an image of Skrikes Wood in a long-ago summer. There, hidden amongst bracken and foxgloves and the trunks of trees, she saw the outline of herself and Mrs. March.

Wyn hurried outside after the boy, snow driving into her face. She called out to Tawhir, but he just kept walking. Not far ahead, where the ice had been smashed up and hollowed, Wyn saw Tawhir stop and look down.

When she caught up with him, she gasped.

Suspended in the heart of the reservoir was the blue-eyed woman the trees had shown her. She lay perfectly still, her long silver hair motionless around a simple blue dress. Her eyes and her lips were fully open, as if she'd been trying to say something, before being stopped mid-breath.

Fighting back her tears, Wyn knelt down, laying a hand on the ice.

"Naia," she whispered. The frozen water spirit stared back at her.

"She could have left and gone south like so many of her kind, to where the rivers still flow," said Tawhir. "Instead she chose to stay close to him. And he had to watch this happen to her, then wait and hope for the ice to melt so they can be reunited."

Tawhir knelt down beside Wyn, placing his hand on the ice beside hers.

"All that time knowing that the one he loves more than anything in the world is so close to him, and so far away. And there's nothing he can do about it."

Moonlight broke through around them. Tawhir stood up quickly, turning away from her.

"I should go and keep watch," he said.

And suddenly Wyn was desperate for him to stay. She reached out for his hand, but in a swirl of wind Tawhir was gone and once again she was left grasping air.

Wyn was too unsettled to sleep that night.

Over and over, she saw the snowball earth, Naia frozen under the reservoir, and Kate lying in hospital, as pale as Mrs. March had once been. Because of her? Memories of a past life kept flashing through her mind. She was soaring over brightly lit cities, over forests being cut and cleared, over great sweeps of bone-white coral lying dead under warm seas. She felt again the fury of her other life. Fury at what the world she was passing over had once been, and what it had become.

Then she was standing at the entrance to a cave, high above the mountain pass, in a maelstrom of storm and lightning. Huge silver eyes hovered in front of her and she was raging against him, against Sh'en Shiekar. She couldn't hear the words passing between them, but she could remember her despair and anger. She had been the storm, and he had been implacable, unyielding. Try as she might, Wyn couldn't remember why.

In a dale to the north, exhausted from his long run through the snow, the wolf pack leader padded into a barn that lay abandoned on the high moors. Denali waited there, Foehn at his side. Denali bent to greet the wolf, stroking the places where the brambles had bit into his skin. Afterwards, he told Foehn what the wolf had seen, about Wyn fighting off the pack once Thwaite had fallen.

"The girl moved the trees with her mind alone? Then it must be Mugasa reborn," said Foehn. "She is stronger than we thought."

"But she has not come into her true power yet," said Denali. "Is there still no sign of Sh'en Shiekar?"

"He still remains hidden."

"You will find Oya and Sirmik and tell them where the girl is hiding. Together, the three of us will face her."

"The four of us, you mean."

"You must hold back. If we fail, it will be your task to lead the other spirits loyal to our cause."

"I won't let you go without me. What if she becomes Mugasa again, or Sh'en Shiekar comes to her defense?"

Denali took her in his arms.

"In five thousand years, when have I ever lost a fight?"

"No spirit has ever come close to defeating a dragon."

"You're talking about ordinary spirits, and I am not an ordinary spirit. There will be three of us, striking from all sides. All it will take is for one of us to get through their defenses. But it may not come to this. The girl may not become Mugasa and Sh'en Shiekar may be on the other side of the world, for all we know.

"We're close, Foehn, so close to ending their foolish rule. We will rid the earth of the human canker that afflicts her and see new spirits born in every territory once more. Imagine it — the second age of the spirits. I've dreamt of this time for too long to let it slip from our grasp."

"If Mugasa does not return before tomorrow night, do you still believe Sh'en Shiekar will sacrifice himself?"

"He has no choice. He will cross the boundary, just as she did."

20

❖❖❖❖

Clouds, blood-red in the setting sun. The snow-capped mountains. Glittering teeth. Huge talons reached for her. He was trying to drag her back to earth, but she wrested herself free, flying upwards towards the shimmering wall of light.

Wyn woke with a start on the thyme floor of Thwaite's house, her heart racing from her dream.

The earth spirit was looking down at her. He looked paler and leaner, but he was himself again and Wyn was so relieved that she got to her feet and hugged him. Thwaite didn't exactly hug her back, but instead squeezed her shoulder, just as Robin always did, and gave her a brief, warm smile.

And then her thoughts turned to Tawhir.

"He's trying to slow down our visitors," said Thwaite, reading her mind.

He told Wyn the news that the blackbirds had delivered. At dawn, Denali had crossed into the northern dales on a direct path to Nidderdale. The fire and ice spirits were also converging on the dale. Wyn felt sick, but did her utmost to keep her voice steady.

"How long?"

"Mid-morning, perhaps dinnertime if the boy has some talent."

The earth spirit took down an axe from the hawthorn wall that was almost as tall as he was and gripped it in his huge hands. Wyn saw that even in the few days she had known him, the earth spirit had aged and grown weaker. His eyes had lost their intense green. There was a stiffness about the way he moved, as if the cold had at last found its way into his bones. Wyn knew that he didn't stand a chance against the rebel spirits, but he would take them on anyway. He would defend her and his territory with whatever strength was left in him.

"The last day of summer," he said. "Are you going to fight for us, child?"

"I'll try."

When the earth spirit smiled, Wyn was reminded of Mrs. March, close to the end.

"We'll both try, and see what comes of it," he said.

Pip was barking from outside the hawthorn house. As the collie ran inside, her coat flecked in snow, Thwaite's blackbirds flew in over her head. They landed on the earth spirit's shoulders, chattering and winking. Wyn understood them, just as Thwaite did.

All around the reservoir, trees bent in the coming storm. Snow drove across the ice. The great storm that had encompassed the world was finally coming to the dale. A man and a woman were coming towards Thwaite's house, both barefoot. The woman was as tall and lean as the beech staff she swung in front of her. In contrast the man was almost as wide as he was short, his face as deeply creased as limestone. While the woman struggled a little with the deep snow, the man stamped through it as if it didn't exist.

"Hackfall and Old Mal," Thwaite told Wyn. "Eight thousand years old and he's convinced he's still green-limbed. Past his prime he may be, but he's still by far the strongest earth spirit in the Dales."

"I thought you couldn't trust them," said Wyn.

"I've no choice, not against the odds we face," muttered the earth spirit, tightening his grip on the shaft of his axe. "Stay by me."

Old Mal marched up and stood with his hands in the pockets of his stained coat, his brilliant green eyes flicking between his fellow earth spirit and Wyn.

"Now then, Thwaite," he said.

"Mal."

Hackfall followed, stepping up to Thwaite to kiss his cheek. Wyn saw her glance towards the center of the reservoir.

"Naia?" she asked gently. Thwaite shook his head.

"Your birds said you needed us in a hurry," said Old Mal. "Said the rebel spirits were after you. Now I see why. What's your name, child?"

"Wyn," she replied, refusing to let herself be intimidated by the force of his stare.

"No, your real name. It's Mugasa, I take it."

"Thwaite, is this true? She's the reborn fire dragon?" said Hackfall.

"Not yet, she isn't, or why else would he be greeting us with knuckles white on his axe?" said Mal. "Worried we might have joined those damned fool rebels, are you, Thwaite? I may be old, but I've not lost my wits entirely. What about you, Hackfall?"

The female earth spirit smiled warmly at Wyn.

"Welcome back, Mugasa," she said. "All these years I have prayed for your return."

While Thwaite told the two earth spirits about how he'd become aware of Wyn, her thoughts returned to the dream she'd woken from in the morning. She saw Sh'en Shiekar clearly now and heard the roar of his voice, calling for her to turn back. But most of all she felt the rage forcing her on. A blind rage that knew nothing but itself. Why? What had she been so angry about?

Hackfall was saying his name.

"What of Sh'en Shiekar. Is there no sign of him?"

"None," said Thwaite.

"It's strange that the wind spirit found her, and her soulmate has not been able to."

Old Mal gave a grunt of agreement.

"There's much here that doesn't make sense. But we should be on with doing, not going about in circles. The fire and ice spirits we should be able to handle. If it truly is Denali with them, that's another matter. It'll take all of us and the wind spirit to hold him off. Though I doubt we can do more than that. Only a dragon could bring him down."

The brilliant green eyes returned to Wyn.

"It'll be up to you, Mugasa, or if not you then Sh'en Shiekar."

"You don't have to do this," she said.

"These are our dales, and I'll not have outsiders coming and thinking they can do as they like here," said Old Mal.

Both Thwaite and Hackfall were nodding.

"Where will we face them, Thwaite?" asked Hackfall.

"The reservoir would give the ice spirit too much to work with, likewise the woods for the fire spirit. Our best chance is open ground. The wind spirit will be of most use there." Thwaite pointed his axe uphill. "We'll face them on the tops, on Fountain's Earth Moor."

Thwaite led the way at a ferocious pace up the side of the dale, through the ever-strengthening storm. Pip wasn't with them. Before their climb, Thwaite had told the collie to gather the other animals from his house and lead them to the cavern.

Thwaite was struggling in the deep snow, constantly driving his axe into the ground and pulling himself on. Hackfall, too, was relying on her staff. Old Mal plowed on, hands in his pockets, as if he were treading the short grass of spring. Just like him, Wyn barely noticed the snow. As they climbed, the lights of all the villages of Nidderdale were coming into view: Wath, Pateley, Bewerley, Glasshouses and all the others, strung at intervals on the road to the distant glow of Harrogate. Her eyes cut through distance and the storm, picking out Mrs. March's old house, Highdale, and John's house, on to Harrogate where Kate still lay in a hospital bed.

They were all the people in the world that she cared about. Could she rediscover the power to save them? Even as she swore that she would, the old, wild voice rose up inside her, telling her to leave them to their fate. Confused and angry, Wyn snapped her gaze skyward. Tawhir was up there, somewhere. She sensed him watching her.

When they reached the moor, the earth spirits huddled together, discussing how best to defend against the rebel spirits.

"Not a cavern. We'd risk getting trapped," said Thwaite.

"It has to be an enclosure," said Hackfall, "with walls to keep out fire and ice."

"Denali will do his best to break them. At least two of us will have to be renewing them constantly," said Thwaite.

"That'll be you and Wyn. Now, let's be on with it," said Old Mal, bending to the ground and pushing his hands under the snow. Wyn watched Thwaite and Hackfall copy him. The ground began to shake, and in a large ring around them, black stalks of heather were rising up from the whiteness. After them, with a great creaking and rumbling, came earth and rock, yards thick. First ankle height, then waist height. By the time the walls of the enclosure were above Wyn's shoulders, blood had started to weep from Thwaite's wound, staining his tweed coat. Thwaite took no notice of it.

"Stop it," Wyn told him. The earth spirit ignored her. "Just stop!" she insisted, kneeling down next to him and dragging his hands from the ground. The wall trembled and slowed fractionally.

"Are you trying to kill yourself?" she demanded, drawing back Thwaite's coat and pressing her hand against the wound. As the blood seeped through her fingers, Wyn pressed harder, feeling a strange new energy build in her body and surge down her arms, into her hands. Now, instead of blood, there was a golden glow between her fingers and the earth spirit gave a deep sigh. Glancing up, she saw that his eyes had grown greener. When she removed her hands, the wound was healed and a trace of gold clung to his skin.

"Thank you," said Thwaite, and there was a little wonder in his expression. Old Mal and Hackfall were both watching her.

"Maybe you'd like to give us some help?" said Old Mal, and as Wyn knelt beside the other earth spirits and pressed her hands to the ground, she was filled with the same new energy. She felt the rocks immediately respond to her, rising from the ground at twice the speed as before. The enclosure rose up, tall as a house.

"Without touch," Thwaite told her, lifting her hands from the ground.

And now, as she stood up and concentrated on the enclosure, her thought reached out for the rocks and they reacted to her, just as before. She had fashioned steps up the inside of the enclosure, and was forging a broad platform to ring the top of it, when in her mind's eye she saw three spirits stepping onto the northern edge of the moor. A dark woman, a pale man, but above all the huge figure with hair falling below his shoulders. Even from a mile distant, she felt his immense power. Beside her, Thwaite was looking in the same direction, hands tightening around his axe.

A second later, her heart raced as Tawhir hurtled down into the enclosure, his flowing hair matted with snow and ice.

"They're here," he gasped.

21

⬧⬧⬧⬧

Wyn stood on the stone battlements, flanked by Thwaite and Tawhir. Hackfall and Old Mal waited outside the enclosure, Hackfall poised with her staff, Old Mal motionless as rock, hands in his pockets.

"If we can't stop them, you're to fly her out of here. Take her to Etna or one of the other great fire spirits," Thwaite told Tawhir.

"She will find her strength," said Tawhir. "Won't you, Mugasa?" He was standing very close to her now, his clothes and hair covered almost completely in snow. There was a wildness to his voice that she hadn't heard before. He looked older and far more dangerous than she remembered him.

He rose into the air, wind billowing around him.

Denali and the others were walking towards them. They stopped a hundred yards from the enclosure. The huge earth spirit looked directly at Wyn and she would have fallen backwards if Thwaite hadn't gripped her arm.

"You're stronger than him," said Thwaite.

"I'm not. He's …"

"Just a spirit. You were born to rule the spirit world."

The pale man was walking forward, eyes gleaming white, and Wyn watched with wonder as the snow froze in the sky overhead. The heavy flakes bonded together, growing into long shards of ice. With a cry, the pale man thrust his arms towards the enclosure and the shards were raining down around them. Just in time, Thwaite tore a huge slab of rock from the wall of the enclosure, holding it over them. The shards dashed against the rock. As they did, Wyn caught sight of Tawhir dodging this way and that. Below them Hackfall was dashing the ice with her staff, while Mal was holding two stone clubs and beating the shards away.

Now the fighting began in earnest, and all around her Wyn saw fire and ice and felt the earth shaking. The dark-skinned woman was running forward, her robes wreathed in flame, and Tawhir was coming at her head-on, driving the middle winds into her. Hackfall was on her knees, one hand on the ground, fending off the ice spirit. As ice washed over her staff, the ground opened up around the pale man, dragging him down, but slowly, too slowly. Ice was fastening onto Hackfall's hands, rising up her shoulders.

Casting aside his clubs, Old Mal pounded towards the ice spirit, tearing him from Hackfall. The two spirits gripped each other like wrestlers and Wyn saw for the first time the immense strength of the old earth spirit and heard the ice spirit's cry, before he slumped to the ground.

But even as Old Mal was helping Hackfall to her feet, the fire spirit had risen into the sky and was swirling around and around, flames streaking out from her like the rays of the sun. She saw Tawhir dodge and weave, still driving the middle winds at her, refusing to draw back even as the fire spirit was advancing on him. A bolt of fire just missed his face. Wyn saw another catch his jacket. She threw her will into the sky, desperately trying to summon stronger winds to help him, but before she could, the boy was struck by a firebolt in the chest. As he was flung backwards, another bolt hit him on the arm, sending him spinning to the ground.

Wyn screamed and would have jumped down from the enclosure if Thwaite hadn't held her back.

"No," he rasped. "Mal will help him. Bring down the winds. Stop the fire spirit."

Wyn pushed Thwaite away and leapt down onto the snow. She reached Tawhir just as Old Mal did. The boy was an ashen color, but awake.

From the corner of her eye, Wyn saw the fire spirit still whirling overhead. Hackfall, her face still frosted with ice, was tracking Oya's every move with her staff. Thwaite hurried up and stood over Wyn, his axe at the ready.

"Keep back," he told her. But Wyn was in no temper for hiding. All her thoughts were bent on the fire spirit. Rising to her feet, she threw her will into the sky. The day before, on Eagle Rock, she'd only just been able to call down the middle winds. Now they came to her command without hesitation. Wyn yelled up at the skies, summoning the middle winds by name in a voice that she barely recognized as her own.

And they heard her. Down they came. Down into the dale. With all the fury within her, she drove them at the fire spirit. They tore into Oya and carried her away with them, back into the heavens.

Only Denali remained. As he strode towards Wyn, the moor shook as if it was being torn apart by an earthquake. Behind her, the enclosure was reduced to rubble.

Thwaite, Old Mal and Hackfall had dropped to the ground, trying to calm the earthquake. The shaking lessened fractionally, but now the earth was opening up around them. Snow and earth tumbled into the darkness of fissures. The ground split under Hackfall. As she fell, her staff suddenly became a young tree, its branches reaching skyward. Old Mal threw himself to one side, managing to catch the uppermost branches.

Another fissure was opening up right under Thwaite.

"Don't you dare!" rasped the earth spirit, slamming one hand onto the ground. But even as the fissure reluctantly closed, another was opening up beside him. Again Thwaite silenced it.

"They can't stop Denali," shouted Tawhir, getting unsteadily to his feet.

As he spoke, Denali was raising his hands. Columns of rock rose up from the ground. Jagged edges grew from them and it took Wyn a moment to see what they were — brambles made of rock. They reached toward her like snakes.

"Mugasa!" yelled Tawhir.

Wyn stepped forward to meet the twisting rock. Power, strength, heat grew in her, wave after wave, multiplying over and over, until Wyn was shaking from the force of it.

A golden light was growing around her.

Wyn saw the huge earth spirit frown. The rocky brambles were almost upon her.

"Now, Mugasa!" yelled Tawhir.

Throwing her hands wide, Wyn released the power inside her. The rocks burned gold, then shattered.

They lay, smoldering, on the ground.

Tawhir was yelling at her, telling her to make the smoldering rocks jump into flames, but try as she might, she couldn't create fire. She felt as though she was being torn in half.

And then the dale vanished around her and she was in the skies above the mountains, face to face with a glittering dragon. She fell to her knees on the snow of the moor, oblivious to new rock thorns emerging from the ground around her. This time they were smaller and moved far more quickly.

She was oblivious to Thwaite's warning shout.

The thorns coiled around her body, biting into her.

Now everything was a blur of pain. Denali was advancing. Hackfall and Old Mal were standing between her and the rebel spirit. Thwaite was trying to tear the thorns from Wyn. Only Tawhir was motionless, a single tear running down his angular face as he watched her.

When Denali was just a few paces away, Hackfall and Old Mal grappled with him. Hackfall was sent tumbling across the snow almost immediately, but Old Mal held his ground against his huge adversary, beating away the rock thorns that rose up to bind him, stamping bare feet to silence the earth when it began opening up around him. For a brief moment Wyn thought Old Mal might be strong enough to hold Denali off. To her dismay, the mountain lord drove forward, pulling one of Old Mal's clubs free, and with a shocking force, he smashed it against Old Mal's head.

The old earth spirit collapsed.

Now only Thwaite stood between Denali and her, holding out his axe in front of him.

"Move away from her, Brother," said Denali, still breathing hard from his fight with Mal.

"Never," said Thwaite.

"The time of the dragons is over. You know this."

Thwaite glanced back at Wyn. His face was a mask of sweat and exhaustion. He gave her the faintest of nods, then he was spinning around, sweeping his axe at the huge earth spirit.

As if he were swatting away a fly, Denali smashed the axe with one of Old Mal's clubs. Thwaite was dragged away by thorns of rocks.

Denali towered over Wyn, raising the clubs to strike her.

"Forgive me, Mugasa," he said. "You believed in our cause. But only your death can make it a reality."

The clubs swept down towards her, but when they were only inches from her neck, Tawhir was suddenly beside her, catching the clubs in his bare hands.

The clubs shattered. A circle of fire formed around Denali, burning with a silver flame.

Wyn saw the shock in the earth spirit's face.

"You," he gasped.

The silver fire wrapped around Denali. Tawhir raised his hands and the earth spirit was raised up above the moor.

"It's too late," said Denali. "She won't return for you."

The circle of fire blazed with renewed power, and then it was gone. The great earth spirit fell to the moor.

Now the boy Wyn had known as Tawhir turned to face her. Silver light poured off him, and Wyn could see the glittering diamond scales beneath his skin.

Sh'en Shiekar, the ice dragon.

22

All the memories of a thousand, thousand years swept through her.

Wyn remembered her past life and the life before it and on, further and further into the past, to when the world was young and she rose up over it for the first time, with him. He was in every memory, in berry-bright autumns and beside all the torrents of spring.

And now she remembered why they had fought.

For hundreds of years, she had seen the hurt that humans were causing the natural world and had wanted to use her power to punish them. But at every turn he had blocked her, insisting that they leave humans alone. They were born of the earth, just like all other creatures, he had said. As dragons, it was their duty to guide and nurture all of the earth's children, not wage war against them. Only the earth herself could act against them, he told her.

But as the years had passed and the destruction of the humans had grown worse, many spirits had begun to take matters into their own hands, battering towns and cities with flooding, hurricanes, snowstorms and great wildfires. To Wyn's fury, Sh'en Shiekar had intervened on the side of humans, using all his power to beat back the spirits. Not wanting to fight Sh'en Shiekar, she had flown beside him. But with every passing year, her anger towards humans and Sh'en Shiekar had mounted.

And secretly, more and more spirits had united, with one aim in mind — to kill the dragons and then, unchallenged, to take revenge on humankind.

As the rebellion had grown, Wyn had tried to make Sh'en Shiekar realize that their time was over. For tens of thousands of years, the dragons had watched over the balance of nature and kept the peace among spirits. Now it was time for them to give up their watch and to give the spirits free rein. Finally, she and Sh'en Shiekar could lead mortal lives, grow old and have children of their own.

But Sh'en Shiekar had refused to listen to her, even when she had learned of a way for them to give up their powers. Nothing would dissuade him. They must protect all the earth's children, humans and spirits alike, for as long as the earth needed them, he told her.

Wyn had finally resolved to take matters into her own hands. She would give up her own powers and live a mortal life. Whatever happened, whatever the consequences, she would remain mortal and wait for Sh'en Shiekar to join her.

Set on her course, she had streaked upwards into the sky.

Knowing what she was attempting, he had tried to stop her, tried to bring her back to earth. But she had flown into the sky, faster than all the winds, faster than the setting sun, faster even than him. At the highest reaches of the sky, she had crossed the shimmering border between the earth and the darkness of space.

Now, on the snows of Nidderdale, disbelief and anger were written across Sh'en Shiekar's face.

"Have you lost your mind, Mugasa?" he demanded. "You would still sacrifice yourself and the earth rather than return to power?"

"You lied to me. You treated all of us like fools."

"I had spent years searching for you and when at last I found you, you didn't recognize me. We have always been together, Mugasa, from the moment the earth created us, and you acted like I was a stranger."

Angrily, Wyn shook her head.

"You didn't want me to know you. You wanted to trick me into returning to power, without me remembering what had passed between us, or the oath I had sworn."

"You turned your back on the world, Mugasa."

"You were afraid."

"Yes, I was afraid! I was afraid of what would happen if we tried to give up our powers. Look what your absence has done to the world."

"It's not my fault the world has grown cold. You tried to make me think that, but it wouldn't have happened if you'd followed me across the border."

In her anger, Wyn didn't notice that Thwaite and Hackfall were silently watching the argument between them. Hackfall was holding Old Mal's head in her lap.

"Of all the forms the earth could have chosen, she brought you back as a human. She wanted you to learn to care for them, just as she does. But even now, you would see them wiped off the face of the world."

"I don't, I …" began Wyn, her thoughts turning to Kate, Robin, John and above all Mrs. March. But then the great, wild voice rose up in her; the voice of who she had been, of Mugasa. All the old hatred and mistrust of humans was in that voice. Wyn broke off, rubbing the tears running down her face with her sleeve.

"You stood by and let the ice bear hurt Kate. You could have healed her, but you didn't."

"I can take the ice from her, but only you can save her and all the other humans. There's still time," said Tawhir, reaching out and holding her tightly.

"I can't," she said.

Tawhir released her.

"Then stay hidden. If the earth brings me back, maybe you will look for me, as I did for you," he said.

His eyes glimmered sliver.

"Your friend is healed."

He was gone.

"Tawhir!" she cried. There was no trace of him in the sky.

Far off, the silence of the dale was shattered by a chainsaw roaring into life. Another joined it. And another. Even though she was several miles away, Wyn felt the trees in Skrikes Wood vibrating. She could sense their fear. Angrily, she tore her thoughts away from Tawhir. Only now did she turn her attention to the three earth spirits.

Old Mal lay motionless in the snow. She bent over him. "I'll see to him," Hackfall told her.

The look on her face was plain, just as it was on Thwaite's. Wyn didn't have to be a mind reader to know what they were thinking, what they thought of her.

"We need to stop the felling," she told Thwaite.

He was looking between her and the sky, searching for the boy who she could no longer sense.

"You should go after him."

"I can't. I'm not Mugasa anymore."

"No, you're Wyn. You're better than she was. Mugasa made a choice to abandon the world. Will you make that choice again?"

Frustration raged in Wyn. She couldn't stop Tawhir and bring back summer, but she could at least save Skrikes Wood. She turned away from the earth spirits, breaking into a run.

"Well, are you coming?" she yelled over her shoulder.

Wyn led Thwaite at a fierce pace towards the wood. With every step through the snow, more memories of her past came back to her. Over and over, she saw woods being cleared and houses being built, great rivers dammed, the smoke of a million chimneys rising into the sky. And she saw Sh'en Shiekar and herself arguing in the mountain tops.

But even as she worked herself up into a rage, Wyn heard Mrs. March's strident voice, Kate's laughter, and felt Robin's hand squeezing her shoulder.

Where was Tawhir now? When would he cross the border? Would he wait until the last moment, when the sun was setting, or attempt it now?

Pateley Bridge was vanishing under the driving snow. The streets were empty. All the lights in the houses were off. Candles glimmered behind windows.

Thwaite drove the butt of his axe into the snow in front of him, pulling himself on through the storm.

"I should have known the boy was Sh'en Shiekar," he said. "Who else could have found you?"

"He should have said who he was."

"If he gives up his powers, the weather will return to normal, but it won't last. The rebel spirits will cause chaos, and don't think humans will take things lying down."

Wyn saw John. He was in the upper reaches of Skrikes Wood, standing beside his father, as David Ramsgill oversaw a tall birch being felled. Without replying to Thwaite, she hurried towards the roar of chainsaws.

The men started when they saw her stride out towards them. David Ramsgill waved his arms, shouting at them to turn off their saws. Snow flurried over fallen trees.

"Wyn! Where have you been? I've been trying to reach you for days," called John, running forward to greet her.

"I thought you wanted to stop the felling, not join in with it," she snapped.

The boy flushed.

"You're to go back home, Wyn," said David Ramsgill. "It's not safe for you to be here."

"I'm not leaving until the felling stops."

"John, take your friend home."

Nervously, John reached out for Wyn. She slapped his hand away. The boy winced, looking at her in surprise.

From the corner of her eye, she saw Thwaite, leaning on his axe at the edge of the clearing. He couldn't stop the felling. He wouldn't.

Angrily, Wyn sent her thoughts down into the ground. Down beneath the snow, the frozen soil, deep into the rocky bones of the dale. They were reluctant to listen to her, but she would have none of it. Grasping the rocks with her will, Wyn forced them into life.

All across the wood, the ground began shaking; a low rumble at first, causing John, his father, and the other men to step back, alarmed. At Wyn's command, the shaking grew stronger and now snow was tumbling from trees, the fallen birches crashing into each other. John, David Ramsgill and his men were struggling to stay on their feet. Wyn saw Thwaite drop to his knees, placing his hands on the snow. She felt his will trying to compete with her own, trying to calm the earth. Wyn increased the strength of the earthquake, dominating the earth spirit's power as if it barely existed.

The slim birches still standing at the top of the wood were swaying furiously now. But Wyn was oblivious to their voices, to the sound of tearing roots.

As Thwaite fought against her, one of his blackbirds jinked through the falling snow. The bird was followed by Robin, coming uphill through the wood on his hands and knees.

He had almost reached Thwaite when several of the birches were ripped from the ground. Wyn saw them falling towards Robin, saw him look up in alarm.

Then, just inches from Robin, Thwaite caught them in his huge hands.

Wyn stumbled backwards, shocked at what had almost happened. She felt John's hands steadying her.

"You okay?" he asked. Wyn nodded. As she did, all her senses came to life.

A soft wind began to blow through the tree tops. A faint music rose up from the canopy as one by one the trees found their voices. Wyn searched the sky for Tawhir, but he wasn't causing the wind. All through Skrikes Wood, trees were breaking into song; the low burr of hollies and oaks, rising through pine and beech, to the bell-like chiming of birches. Wyn saw David Ramsgill staring up at the trees, wonder written across his face. Several of his men were doing the same, as was John.

"What is that?" he asked Wyn.

"You can hear it?"

"It sounds like … singing."

Wyn nodded at the boy. The trees had found their voices, but not because of anything she had done. Just for a moment, another presence had come into the wood, filling everything with warmth and light. Wyn's eyes met Thwaite's and she saw his joy. As the spirit of the earth herself vanished and the trees fell silent, Wyn hugged her arms to her chest, letting the tears fall freely down her face.

"Wyn, love?"

It was Robin. She let him put his arms around her.

"I heard from the hospital. Kate's woken up."

David Ramsgill was still looking up into the trees. Some of his men had put down their chainsaws, while others still held theirs, and were asking if they should resume felling.

"No, you mustn't," said Robin.

"Are you going to petition me again, Robin?" asked David Ramsgill.

"If I have to."

John's father's expression changed. He was looking directly at Thwaite now. Wyn saw the earth spirit nod in greeting.

"Who on earth...?" he muttered. Wyn squared up in front of David Ramsgill.

"When you were a boy, you could feel and see things when you were outside in the woods and fields. Things that other people couldn't," she said.

"I don't know what you're saying, Wyn," he replied, glancing between her and Thwaite.

"Just because you have ignored this gift for years, doesn't mean you don't still have it."

Thwaite slipped behind trees. David Ramsgill was shaking his head in disbelief.

"What gift? Wyn?" John was asking.

"Call off your men, David," said Robin.

John's father nodded, slowly.

"What is it, Dad?"

"We'll come back another day."

He put his arm around his son. With a final curious look backwards, he strode out amongst his men, telling them that the felling was off.

23

"It's madness. You don't even know where he is," said Robin.

But Wyn did, with absolute certainty.

"He's in the Alps," she said.

"If Thwaite's right, there'll be spirits all over the world looking for you. The moment you leave the dale, you'll be exposed."

"I can outrun them."

"Can you, child?" said Thwaite. "Are you ready to become who you were born to be?"

Wyn wasn't ready. She was terrified of what lay before her, but for the first time her mind and heart spoke as one and she knew what she had to do. She did her best to hide her fear from Robin and Thwaite.

"I can try," she said, sending her thought into the sky.

To her embarrassment, Thwaite lowered himself onto one knee, bowing his head to her.

"Fly well, Wyn," called Thwaite above the howl of the coming winds. Tears were filling Robin's eyes.

Then the winds came screaming through the trees. At the last moment, Wyn realized that she had no idea how this was going to work. Hoping for the best, she stuck out her arms like birds' wings.

Fists slammed into her. She tumbled head over heels through the air, out of the wood and up the side of the dale. All around her the winds howled with something like laughter. At a command of "Stop!" Wyn was thrown facedown into a snowdrift, her breath knocked out of her. The winds fled upwards as Wyn stumbled to her hands and knees and threw up.

She had landed in the moors at the edge of Nidderdale. Far away, the winds were still shrieking at their sport. Angrily, Wyn rose to her feet and wrested back the middle winds. They came faster than before, and this time she made them carry her how she wanted. It was like she was surfing and the winds were waves that she had to learn to ride. The winds obeyed her will, although not without some ideas of their own.

They nudged her towards the deep recesses of the storm, all the time whispering about the wild fun of dodging lightning and outpacing thunder.

She was flying! Really flying! On her own, without Tawhir to hang on to. The winds offered her ever more speed and she took it, greedily. Yelling them on, she streaked east, deeper into the vast snowstorm that was growing stronger and colder by the second.

Beneath her, Wyn watched towns come and go; pools of orange light in the frozen landscape. Every so often, the vast poly-farms appeared, miles upon miles of crops visible through the plastic sheeting that covered them.

And occasionally against the snowy landscape, Wyn caught sight of spirits.

She saw earth spirits, sometimes in human form, other times as animals. But in whichever form they took, Wyn found she recognized the earthers as clearly as if they were bathed in green light. She saw water spirits frozen in lakes and rivers, just as Naia had been. Far off, where the coast met the frozen sea, she saw a wind spirit with flaming red hair, who Wyn knew as Landlash. He watched her pass with suspicious, gleaming eyes.

As she streaked across the pale sea, reaching mainland Europe, Wyn had the sense of the world shrinking around her. With a glance, distant landscapes were suddenly close up. Each new place seemed utterly familiar. She remembered the faces of the spirits who lived there, past and present. She knew all their allegiances, their rivalries and their disputes over territory. It felt like a million voices were clamoring in Wyn's head.

Suddenly, the middle wind that was carrying her swept away, back towards England, and Wyn fell hundreds of feet before another wind swept underneath and caught her.

"Come back!" Wyn shouted at the departing wind.

But no command would make this wind return.

"It's at the end of its range," said a voice sharply. A stern-looking girl in pale swirling robes materialized just in front of Wyn. The name, Foehn, came immediately to Wyn's mind.

"The middle winds always weaken. Then even the most powerful wind spirits are vulnerable. That is, if you are a wind spirit."

She smiled at Wyn. A thin, fleeting smile, trying to mask the hatred in her face.

"Get out of my way," said Wyn, all the time searching the skies for another middle wind. There was one to the west. She summoned it.

"Tell me your name."

"Wyn."

"No, your real name."

"My name's Wyn."

Foehn drew away from Wyn, her eyes gleaming gray.

"Sh'en Shiekar isn't here to save you now, Mugasa."

Through the gathering storm Wyn saw three spirits tearing towards her: two ice spirits in the form of eagles, with feathers of snow and talons of ice, and Landlash, his whole body crackling with lightning.

Just in time, the middle wind swept in from the west. Wyn drove it at the birds. One of the eagles was sent tumbling back into the storm, but the other ice spirit was too fast. The eagle swept under Wyn, then shot up, talons outstretched, and gripped her legs. Wyn cried out and tried to beat the bird off with her fists and the winds. But even as Wyn commanded winds to blast against the birds, Foehn and Landlash were trying to take control of them.

The first eagle returned, slamming into Wyn. All she felt was pain as both ice spirits attacked her with talons and beaks.

Locked in her battle with the four spirits, Wyn tumbled downwards. She was fighting for her life, in a blur of snow and blood and anger … anger that she would die like this, anger that she wouldn't be able to reach Tawhir. Wyn lashed out against the spirits, her fingers prising loose talons even as she felt the winds returning to her control. She was no longer falling. And the storm no longer raged around her. A blue corridor had opened up overhead, rising all the way up to the distant mists of the upper skies.

Moving across them, like vast torrents, Wyn sensed the high winds.

Reaching up her thought, she summoned them to her. The high winds didn't shift their course or even seem to notice her. Wyn heard Tawhir's voice berating her.

"You ruled the winds!" Wyn yelled up at the skies, calling the high winds by name.

And now they heard her. Down, down came the mighty torrents of the skies. Foehn gave a shriek of rage and then she and the other spirits were flung aside as the dragon winds snatched Wyn away and hurtled her through the storm and up, up, into the stratosphere.

She raced beneath the cloak of space.

Unlike the middle winds that fell away after a short time, the high winds carried her across mountain ranges, forests and cities without once losing speed. Only after what seemed like an age did Wyn have to summon other high winds to carry her onwards.

The last day of summer was aging around her.

She streaked across Europe until she saw mountains, their golden peaks rising above the wild weather. The storm that had covered the world had yet to touch them. Praying that this meant Tawhir was there, Wyn hurtled towards them.

She had flown through these mountains a thousand times in her dreams. Releasing the high winds, Wyn summoned middle winds to carry her among them, steering a path that led towards a remote valley,

As she drifted over the valley, Wyn's heart began to pound. She had always thought of Nidderdale as her home, but now that she was here, she realized that this was where she truly belonged.

Everything she looked for was there: the three peaks with the glacier between them; the small lake, now frozen hard; and the pine forest, like a vast white canopy. She picked out familiar individual trees. Was it the wind bending them, or did the trees lean towards her?

Above the forest was a wide slope leading to the lake. Once it had been a wildflower meadow. How many times in her dreams had she flown amongst the flowers and felt them brush against her belly?

Her gaze turned to the tallest of the three peaks. She flew towards it, towards the cave of her dreams that looked out over the world.

Wyn had crossed half of Europe in the hope that Tawhir would be there. Now she concentrated on the cave, trying to see into it.

Wyn landed on the wide snowy ledge outside the cave, slipping a little as she caught her balance. Icicles, glowing pink in the setting sun, hung down over the cave mouth. Wyn's senses strained for any sound or movement from within. There was only darkness and silence. Praying that she would find Tawhir inside, Wyn stepped out of the storm.

23

❖❖❖❖❖

"Tawhir!"

Her voice echoed around the empty cave.

A film of dust lay over everything, resting like snow over the smooth rock.

She saw herself looking out of the cave one hot summer morning. Wildflowers and lean alpine grass filled the meadow. White-bellied swifts raced around the peaks, where blue gentians clung to sunny precipices like climbers pausing to admire the valley below. In the form of a mountain goat, Tawhir was lying by the edge of the small lake, his eyes shut. Moments later, she was beside him. All that morning, they lay together beside the lake, their minds roaming across the world, watching over the lands and the waters and the skies.

Wyn already knew what she would see when she went to the back wall of the cavern. Nevertheless, she still had to steady herself when she saw what dust or time couldn't obscure.

Worn with age, but unmistakeable, the yin-yang symbol was carved into the rock. Hugging her arms around her chest, Wyn returned to the cave mouth, staring numbly at the snow-filled meadow and the towering fury of the approaching storm.

Night had almost come.

"TAWHIR!" she yelled to the sunset.

She searched the sky but could not sense him. He was either far, far away, or hiding from her.

Sunlight faded. Wind whipped into Wyn's face. Lightning and thunder were all around her. The storm had finally reached the valley, snuffing out the final pocket of clear sky in the world.

The last day of summer was coming to an end.

She wasn't going to abandon the earth, or Tawhir. Wyn had no idea how she was going to transform into a dragon, or even where Tawhir was, but she wasn't going to stay here and watch summer die around her.

Throwing up her will into the storm, she summoned the high winds and hurtled upwards into the maelstrom.

The sky blackened around her.

Stars brightened and swelled. The last moon of summer was rising, hollow with age.

With her eyes and her senses she searched for Tawhir.

She didn't notice the golden shadow that was growing around her, or see the fiery trail in her wake.

Something shimmered far away.

At the edge of space, a mouth grew out of the darkness, then a face with swept-back horns, disappearing into a long neck glittering with diamond scales. Huge silver eyes blinked open. Lightning flashed up and down the length of a swirling body.

The dragon hovered at the border of the world on great, slow-beating wings.

"TAWHIR!" Wyn yelled. And as soon as she spoke his name, she didn't just see the dragon, she also saw the boy who had found her at the skating lake, who had knelt beside her on Thwaite's sleeping platform, looking out at the reservoir. They were one and the same, dragon and boy.

The dragon's silver eyes left her, looking upwards. His wings gathered and released, driving him into the shimmering border.

"NO! TAWHIR!"

Suddenly lightning was exploding all around him. She saw his back arch and his wings twist. Diamond scales were being ripped from his body. But despite his agony, Tawhir was still trying to force his way across the border.

With all the speed she could summon from the high winds, Wyn raced after him.

Now Tawhir was crossing the border. His head broke through, then one wing, and another. Incandescent light filled the sky. Scales fell earthwards like shards of ice. His body was vanishing. Just as Wyn was reaching out to grab hold of his tail, it whipped away from her grasp. Traveling too fast to stop, Wyn smashed into the shimmering wall.

Pain ripped through her. In a shard of sparks she was hurled back from the border. In her shock, Wyn lost control of the winds and fell hundreds of feet before she gathered them to her again.

From the other side of the border, Tawhir was writhing as spasm after spasm shook his huge body. With each spasm more diamond scales were ripped from him, leaving bloody streaks.

Wyn screamed for him to come back, but if the dragon heard her, he didn't show it. He twisted away, heading further into the darkness.

Wyn threw herself at the border. Again the shimmering wall flung her back. The glittering dragon was spinning slowly, scales drifting from his body. His eyelids were closing.

For a third time, Wyn flew at the border, but this time she stopped a fraction before it. Just like Tawhir had done, she tried to fight her way through. Her fingers clawed at the shimmering wall. Sparks of golden light burst around her, and blood poured off her hands.

She scarcely noticed that her body was taking its true form.

In her past life, her scales had been rubies and diamonds and emeralds, the colors of her first dawn in the forests. Now, as she stretched out her new wings, they were marked with the colors of the dale. Citrines for the yellows of celandine and trefoil, amethysts for the purples of foxgloves, opals and sapphires for snowdrops, speedwells and bluebells, and on the tips of her wings sparkled the brown diamonds of water avens.

Wyn's talons ripped at the border, tearing a glittering rent between the earth and space. There was only darkness, the hazy colors of stars and Tawhir.

By the time she reached him, her strength was almost gone. She gripped onto Tawhir. But as she tried to fly back towards the border, her wings barely moved. Everything was silence. The earth, far below her, was a swirl of white.

And suddenly Wyn was back in the cavern, watching the bees flying towards the roof, out to their death in the freezing sunlight. She saw Thwaite's lean face watching her and heard his voice explaining, questioning. And then, one after another in flashes, she saw the animals in the cavern — digging and burrowing, the birds hurrying from branch to branch. One by one, all the people she loved most filled her mind: Robin walking in his quick way up the hill to his church; John leading his horse through the fog; Kate running up the bank and looking down into the frozen Nidd; Mrs. March putting her arm around Wyn as they sat hidden in the high reaches of Skrikes Wood one summer afternoon; and finally she saw Tawhir spinning and leaping on the skating lake as she raced beside him.

They had spent an eternity together, but it still wasn't enough time.

Wyn beat her wings again. Slowly, so slowly, she dragged Tawhir back across the border, into life. Locked together, the two dragons fell from the skies, to earth.

They fell through blackness, through the storm. Tawhir's eyes were still closed. Mountains rose up. They fell through peaks. The two dragons tumbled into the deep snow of the meadow.

24

Wyn woke to the excited calls of jackdaws and the fresh smell of morning. When she tried to stretch out, she found that she couldn't.

She opened her eyes.

Tawhir's face was inches from hers. They were lying on a bed of wildflowers, tangled in each other's arms and legs. Wyn brushed her fingers over the whites and silvers of masterwort and edelweiss, the purples and blues of scabious and gentian. And there, rising up around her legs, were the russet heads of water avens.

As she lay there, Wyn felt the ground vibrating underneath her. It only lasted for a moment, but it was enough for Wyn to understand what the earth was telling her. She and Tawhir would not have to guard the balance of nature forever. One day the earth would set them free. She lay back, staring up at the blue skies, happiness washing over her.

The boy stirred. As he tried to get an arm loose, she rolled over and accidentally bumped Tawhir on his nose.

"Ow," he murmured, opening his eyes.

"Sorry," said Wyn. "Are you all right?"

The boy smiled at her and held her close.

Hand in hand, they scrambled out of the wildflowers to see the day.

Golden rivers of sunshine washed down the mountainsides, spilling into the valley. Streaks of green were appearing in the meadow, tumbling down to the fir forest, where trees were shaking off their winter coats and stretching their arms to the morning.

It was the same story in the valleys as far as the eye could see. A rich haze hung across all the Alps.

"You came back to me," said Tawhir.

The boy squeezed her hand.

"This isn't forever, Mugasa," he said. "One day she will release us."

"I know," she whispered. "By the way, in this life, the name's Wyn."

"Perhaps I'll change mine to Tawhir."

"You should, it suits you."

She let go of his hand. He nodded, understanding. The boy rose up into the sky, glancing up towards the mountain cave.

Wyn walked alone in the meadow, gathering her strength.

Finally, she felt she was ready. She rolled up her sleeves.

Taking a deep breath, Wyn knelt on the damp ground, pushing her hands into the soil. She felt the life within it; the tiny vibrations of innumerable sleeping plants, of roots withered by cold, not just in the valley but beyond and beyond and over seas and other seas and more lands and beyond. Gathering all the power and fire inside her, she released it into the ground. All across the alps, the ground shook. The haze covering the sun melted away. In the valley, the remaining snow disappeared and in clumps and singly, wildflowers rose up through wet grass.

Exhausted, she sat down, breathing hard. Tawhir materialized next to her, his hands slipping into hers.

"We should get going. There's much to do."

"Not quite yet. I need to go back to Nidderdale first."

Tawhir raised an eyebrow.

"To your friends?"

Wyn nodded.

"Don't be long, or I'll have to come looking for you again."

Laughing, Wyn leapt into the air, taking dragon shape in an instant. Wrapping clouds around her, she raced into the sky, every atom of her body singing with the joy of speed and the delight of her true form. Tawhir pursued her and together they flew high and westwards, as a warm autumn day unfurled across the world.

Scarcely an hour later, a mist descended on Harrogate hospital.

It washed over the buildings, the car park and the horse

chestnut trees whose branches tapped against some of the lower windows.

Hurrying as fast as she could without breaking into a run, her bare feet squeaking on the linoleum floor, Wyn made her way to the children's ward. A short while later, Wyn was being led along a corridor by a nurse and then shown into a hospital room. Kate was sitting up in bed, surrounded by Robin, Joan and Lisa.

"Wyn!" she exclaimed. "Where have you been?"

But Kate didn't get an explanation. Wyn was hugging her, tears running down her cheeks.

Later, when she went to get her friend a magazine from the hospital shop, Robin caught up with her in the corridor. Light streamed in through tall windows. One of them had been opened a little, letting in the sound of birdsong.

"You did it, love, didn't you? The weather's turning."

There was something almost fearful about the way Robin was looking at her. Could he see who she was now?

Hating the strange formality that had suddenly come between them, she wrapped her arms around Robin.

Despite Kate's protests that she felt fine, the doctors wanted to keep her in hospital at least until the afternoon.

At lunchtime, telling the others that she would see them at home, Wyn walked out of the hospital in the trainers that the nurses had found for her.

Once again, a mist descended over the hospital and the girl with dark red hair stepped into the shadow of trees and vanished from sight.

Wyn thumped down outside Thwaite's hawthorn house. Just like in the valley in the Alps, trees were shrugging off their white overcoats. In the greatest hurry, plants were all pushing through the softening ground. At a thought from Wyn, betony, harebells and water avens appeared and unfurled in brief minutes. The intoxicating smell of fertility filled the dale. Its very air vibrated with life.

With Pip at his side, Thwaite was sitting beside the reservoir, water lapping against his bare feet. Wyn smiled at the change that had come over the earth spirit. His face was fuller and his cheeks ruddier. Streaks of brown ran though his white hair. He looked ten years younger.

"Not bad, Wyn. Not bad at all," he said.

Rain fell.

Since she'd known him, she'd seen his many moods, from anger and pain to cautious wonder, but never the pure delight on his features now.

A moment later a beautiful woman appeared, her blue robes shimmering around her.

"Naia, there is somebody I'd like you to meet," said Thwaite.

The woman turned her beautiful silvery face to Wyn, smiling in a way that sent tingles down Wyn's spine.

"Thank you," whispered the water spirit, bowing her head a fraction, as she took Wyn's hand and kissed it.

Through rain and sunshine, Naia, Thwaite, Pip and Wyn walked alongside the blue reservoir, towards Wath.

Wyn felt the eyes of the earth and water spirits constantly on her, but they never questioned her about what had happened. In truth, she was in no mood for talking, content to listen to the gentle conversation between the two spirits. Thwaite was telling Naia about his plans for replanting the dale, pointing to banks that he would sow with yarrow, a meadow that wanted more red clover and bird's foot trefoil and hawthorns for the birds and bees. As he spoke, Wyn remembered the earth spirit drawing in his sketch pad beside the fire as snow fell outside his house.

Trees reached out and brushed against Wyn as she passed. Birds darted out to greet her. Thwaite's blackbirds appeared, jealously driving off all other comers. Bees from Skrikes Wood came, buzzing over grass that was just starting to unbend in the sunshine and take the faintest green blush. When even the butterflies from the wood arrived, Wyn had the sensation of being mobbed and knew she was drawing too much attention to herself.

With light winds and gentle commands, she sent the birds, bees and butterflies away and calmed the trees. Then, as if she were weaving an invisible cloak, Wyn shielded her power.

The song of the trees filled Nidderdale, spreading to the next dale and the ones after that and on, on, across seas and continents, until the world echoed to their voices.

25

In the days that followed, snows melted and the earth woke out of a deep sleep and blossomed. Rivers unfroze, and on beaches the sea ice retreated and retreated until nothing but blue swells shifted on the horizon.

Most of the snows had left Nidderdale now. Only a few pockets still clung to the tops. Slowly the heather emerged, dark and wet. In the sunlight and warmth, new buds formed and opened. Through the rest of the dale, the tough little spring trees — hawthorn, blackthorn and the cherries — burst into leaf and flower, quickly followed by the statuesque larches and horse chestnuts. The oaks remained resolutely bare. With just a thought, Wyn could have brought them and every other flower and tree into leaf, but instead she left the last traces of winter to vanish at their own pace.

There was only one place where Wyn allowed herself a little influence.

On the first Sunday that she had returned to Nidderdale, Wyn had slipped away from Highdale at sunrise, and after flying fast and far through the waking gardens of southern England and France, she had come to Mrs. March's old home, her pockets full of flower heads and little splints of wood. She had scattered them in and around the deserted house in Spring Wood and set them to grow. By the second Sunday, when Wyn went to pick a bouquet for her old foster mother's headstone, the house had almost vanished from sight, hidden under a white and purple cascade of wisteria, jasmine and roses.

Flowers had sprung up all over the garden; some of her choosing, others of their own accord. Wyn's heart missed a beat when she noticed a trail of water avens that led from the walled garden, taking a curiously direct path through the garden gate and up to a stile that led into Spring Wood. They reappeared on the other side of the stile, then petered out amongst the trees. Wyn sat down beside the last water aven, running her finger against its russet-colored head, talking softly to the morning.

As much as Wyn longed to be able to tell Kate exactly what had happened on the last night of summer and who she had truly become, Wyn held on to her secret, afraid to expose her friend to any future danger.

Her best friend asked her many times about the green-eyed man who had struggled with the bear on the skating lake. Wyn told Kate that she didn't know him and that she'd never seen him again, and Kate nodded along to this, but a look in her eyes told Wyn that her friend didn't quite believe her. She definitely didn't believe Wyn when she tried to tell Kate that she didn't know where Tawhir was.

"So where is he? I know he didn't leave the dale after the accident," said Kate.

It was the first day of the new school year and once again Wyn and Kate had set off together from Highdale, down the steep hill into Pateley Bridge and then along the river Nidd, which flowed swiftly under the green canopy of alders and the noisy conversation of jackdaws.

They were cutting across the field from the river, heading towards Pateley High. The school was all boxy gray and busy with cars and buses pulling up. Wyn's attention had been distracted by an earthquake that was shaking huge swaths of eastern Russia, breaking up ice-locked plains. Three huge black-bearded earth spirits were causing the quake, which was rapidly getting out of control.

"Who?" asked Wyn, returning to the present.

"Tawhir. John said he saw you with him in Skrikes Wood."

"He went back to the Alps."

"Just like that?"

Wyn nodded. Kate's stare became more quizzical.

"Did anything happen between you two?"

"Nothing much."

"Oh, really? So I guess there must be another reason that you're acting differently these days."

"There's nothing different about me."

They had reached the gate at the end of the field that led onto the road. Wyn opened it and they walked through, joining groups of other schoolchildren who had walked from Pateley Bridge. As they streamed across the road, Wyn saw that John was standing by the entrance to the school with Lisa. He waved at them.

"And what about John?" asked Kate.

"What about him?"

"Do you think that you and him…?"

Wyn shook her head.

"Friends," she said.

"Poor John."

Lisa glanced over her shoulder, then positioned herself between John and them, blocking his view.

"Poor John," repeated Kate, laughing.

But even more than Kate, John seemed to sense the change in Wyn. He didn't ask her out on dates anymore, and he became less awkward around her. The only thing he did press her on was the barefooted farmer that he had glimpsed dimly in the fog in Skrikes Wood. All his energies now went into hunting for Thwaite, and to his obvious delight, he was joined in his quest by his father. Often, as she floated invisible in the clouds above Nidderdale, Wyn would watch John and David Ramsgill going on their long walks, and would listen in on their conversation. Mostly John's father talked about his time as a gamekeeper, passing on to John all that he had learned from his years on the land before he went into business.

The only person Wyn completely confided in was Robin.

One night, when Wyn was standing by the open window in her room, ready to leap out into the darkness, Robin tapped on her door. When she let him in, he simply asked her what had happened when she'd flown from Skrikes Wood on the last day of summer, and Wyn told him everything. All the time that she was talking, Robin said nothing. When she was finished he stood stock-still, breathing deeply.

"You're a ..."

"I'm Wyn. I'm just the same," she said quickly. The shock was lifting from Robin, replaced by giddy excitement.

"I can hardly believe it," said Robin. "All these years I've been telling you this and that and there you are, stronger and older than anyone else."

"I'd forgotten everything."

"And now?"

Wyn smiled at her foster father.

"You're going to be leaving us soon, aren't you, Wyn?"

"I'll always keep coming back."

"Will you do two things for me before you go?" said Robin.

When he told her his first request, Wyn thought carefully before agreeing. She asked him what the second thing was, and this time Wyn couldn't help but smile. Glancing out of the window, she drew down the high clouds over Nidderdale, tightening them so thickly that nothing remained but a white mistiness.

"Ready?" she asked Robin. They were sitting on the windowsill. The priest nodded. She put her arm tightly around him. And leapt out into the night.

Wyn fulfilled her other promise a few days later.

On a warm evening, Wyn, Robin and Kate walked across the fields to Wath.

"What are we doing here?" Kate asked, as they climbed a wall and dropped down into a field behind the hamlet. Long blades of sorrel came up to their knees.

"You'll see," said Wyn.

John and his father were waiting for them at the entrance to Spring Wood. Both of them were as curious as Kate as to what they were doing there. The questions continued all the way through the wood and as they passed alongside the reservoir that lay bathed in the setting sun.

Robin led them to Thwaite's house. Mary Hebden and Brian Davis were already there, laying out a picnic. Her collie was lying on the grass next to Pip and Wyn finally realized why the dogs looked so similar; the older collie was Pip's mother. David Ramsgill greeted them, asking what was going on.

"Someone wants to meet you," said Brian Davis.

Thwaite came out of his hawthorn house, holding a spade. At first Kate, John and his father squinted uncertainly at the hawthorns. Then their eyes widened as they began to see the earth spirit clearly.

"Is that a ghost?" said David Ramsgill.

"Do I look like a ghost?" asked Thwaite, striding up to them and planting his spade hard into the ground.

"You were in Skrikes Wood, that time on the bridge," said John, glancing at Wyn. "You could see him, couldn't you?"

"Who are you?" asked David Ramsgill. He jumped back in shock as Naia rose up out of the reservoir nearby, her eyes gleaming blue.

Over the picnic, Naia and Thwaite explained a little about themselves and how John, Kate and David Ramsgill could help them in the dale.

"I've seen you often, enjoying my waters," Naia told Kate. "So you can help me check the streams that run into the Nidd and keep them moving, if you like."

Kate nodded delightedly.

"And you can help me," Thwaite told John and David Ramsgill.

Wyn left them, taking the wooden dishes from the picnic to the shore of the reservoir. High on the hill opposite, in the shadow of an ash, she saw Old Mal and Hackfall. Mal's forehead was still bruised where Denali had struck him, but his eyes burned brighter as ever. She sent her thought to them, and Mal raised a hand, and Hackfall her staff in greeting.

There was a noise behind her. John crouched down next to her, taking a plate and rinsing it in the reservoir.

"You're like him, aren't you? And so is that boy, Tawhir."

Wyn glanced up at John.

"It's okay, I won't tell anyone. It's just … at least now I know why."

John gave her one of his smiles, but there was none of the old tension in it, only warmth.

"Friends?" he said.

Wyn smiled back at him.

"Always."

Much later, under heavy stars, Wyn, John and Kate walked back along the river together. Kate was in the middle, her arms around each of their waists. They barely spoke.

Wyn's thoughts were full of Tawhir. She knew the power the dale had over her was fading. In her heart she was starting to accept the shifting nature of things: the seed of a flower blown from hedge to field; a death in one place becoming a life in another. Water didn't stay in the dale, nor did the clouds, nor the winds, nor the birds and animals and plants. The spirit of Mrs. March, which had remained to watch over Wyn, was now gone to another place.

The dale was connected to everything. What happened here was like a grain of sand falling on a beach. As small as it was, the beach trembled when it struck.

But there were other grains of sand, other dales that needed her attention, now more than ever.

It was time to leave.

Acknowledgments

This book owes many debts of gratitude; to family, friends and colleagues. My first thanks to Sally Wofford-Girand for her early support and championing of a new writer. Likewise to the wonderful Jo Unwin, to the ever brilliant Carrie Plitt and most of all to Clare Conville. Agent. Fairy godmother. Festival collaborator. Harbinger of champagne. Hurrah!

My great thanks to Sheila Barry and all the team at Groundwood for their thoughtful, inspiring collaboration. They have made the book far better than I could have hoped.

To my friends and family, in particular Sam Enthoven. Forever power to your tentacles, mate, be they directed at music or books.

To the landscape of Nidderdale and all the people working so hard to support the flora and fauna of our dale.

A special thanks to Raj Rai, Kat Johnson and all the team at Harrogate Hospital for giving my wife and I the best gift of all, our lovely daughters.

And last to my wife Megan. With my love and gratitude for your constant support.